Sun God, Moon Witch

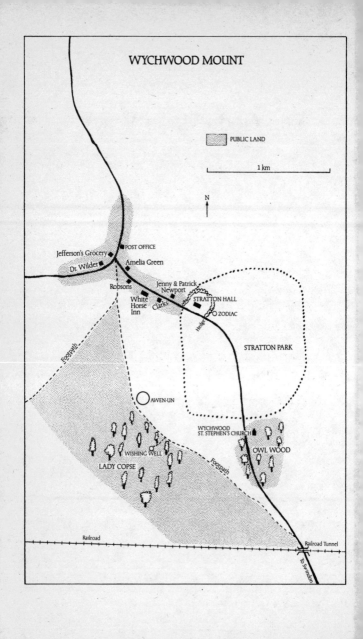

Sun God, Moon Witch

Welwyn Wilton Katz

A Groundwood Book
Douglas & McIntyre
Vancouver/Toronto

Groundwood Books/Douglas & McIntyre
585 Bloor Street West
Toronto, Ontario M6G 1K5

Canadian Cataloguing in Publication Data

Katz, Welwyn
    Sun God, moon witch

ISBN 0-88899-127-4

I. Title.

PS8571.A889S8 1990   jC813'.54   C90-094718-7
PZ7.K37Su 1990

Design by Michael Solomon
Cover art by Paul Zwolak
Printed and bound in Canada

1

Wychwood Mount

"Look out!" The old Austin rattled to a halt, and a middle-aged man dressed in blue jeans and binoculars scurried out of the way. "Did you *see* that fool?" Jenny Newport fumed. "Bad enough parking in a railway tunnel at all, but then to open his door just as I'm trying to squeeze by . . . !" She stuck her head out the window and yelled at the man's back, "Next time you decide to kill yourself, use a pistol!" Then she turned to her niece, her eyes twinkling. "Well, Thorny, how much of his paint do you think we can scrape off?"

Hawthorn McCall poked her head out the window. For the first time since the wedding, she actually felt like smiling. Aunt Jenny was nice. Much nicer than she'd dared to hope. Not that Dad had ever actually said anything; not about Aunt Jenny, anyway. But there had always been something in his voice, as if he were describing French fries instead of his sister . . .

Thorny peered at the car Aunt Jenny was threatening to hit. "I think you're okay," she said shyly, trying to concentrate.

With a dreadful clashing of gears the Austin jerked forward. "Not even a scrape," Aunt Jenny said smugly. "So much for Patrick and his nasty comments about my driving."

Patrick was Aunt Jenny's son. He was the other reason Thorny had been nervous about coming to England. She didn't care if Wychwood Mount itself was small and dull. Most of the time she actually liked quiet places. But what if these unknown relatives of hers didn't want her being dumped on them? Patrick, especially. He was thirteen, Dad had said.

5

What if he hated having her? What if Aunt Jenny was the kind of person who made her kid entertain you? Thorny took a look at her aunt's laughing face under those unruly curls, and relaxed a little. Maybe Patrick would be like his mother. If so, she had nothing to worry about. Nothing in Wychwood Mount, anyway, she amended wryly, thinking of her father and Miriam.

The seat of the old Austin squeaked as they jounced forward, rusty springs protruding. It was very hot in the car. Thorny found herself imagining Miriam in the driver's seat beside her, trying to avoid brushing up against those springs. Miriam again, she scolded herself. She simply couldn't stop thinking about it. She was in for a whole lifetime of good dresses and makeup; of sitting at the dinner table listening to the two of them; of waiting for the moment Miriam thought appropriate to recite the report on her day. It had been bad enough when Miriam and Dad were only just engaged, with her flashing that great big diamond and talking about "our daughter, Hawthorn." What would it be like now that they were married?

"Will you look at that?" Aunt Jenny exclaimed. The engine stalled as she turned around in her seat, waving an expansive arm to her left. There was a field there, open to view, though everything else Thorny had seen had been hedged at the road. It was a wild-looking piece of land with hardly any trees, rising and falling in stone-littered humps, unkempt grass and wildflowers. A path cut across the field, beginning at the side of the railway tunnel they had just come through and disappearing behind one of the little hills. On the path the man they'd almost hit was hurrying to catch up with half a dozen other people. "Press!" he was shouting, waving a notebook.

The people ahead of him didn't seem to hear. The women wore long peasant dresses and had flowers in their hair. Two of them were dancing, while a third walked more sedately between them, holding the hand of a half-naked toddler. There were two men as well. The one in front, some distance ahead of the rest, looked normal. But the second man was wearing a leather tunic and breeches with a pair of stag's antlers strapped to his head. He was shaking a tambourine. Thorny gave her aunt a startled look.

"You may well ask," Jenny nodded. "Fifteen years ago that lot would've called themselves hippies. Now they're pretending to be Morris dancers." She snorted, jabbing at the starter. "It's not as if Wychwood Mount needs any more lunatics," she shouted over the sudden roar of the engine. "What with the ley-hunters and astrologers and newspapermen and all the other quacks—" she grinned, and the car lurched forward "—we probably qualify as the biggest little madhouse in England!"

Thorny frowned over her shoulder at the strange group. "But I thought Wychwood Mount was just a quiet, empty little—" She flushed, realizing how her words sounded.

"Don't worry," Aunt Jenny said. "I've heard it all before. Your father's views are well known."

"It's just that Dad likes big cities," Thorny explained quickly. "He's not the kind to—"

"To flourish in a backwater," her aunt nodded. The sardonic note in her voice surprised Thorny, slight though it was. "Some people can't help being allergic to the dust of ages," Jenny went on more lightly. "And I must admit it is quiet here, or was, anyway, until the lunatics descended on us. Only twelve houses, an inn, the church and the Hall—all quite comfortably populated, but just the same, not exactly a crowd. Of course, Swindon isn't so awfully far. Belman's counting on that for labour for his cement factory."

They were driving now in the shade of a small wood. The trees were enormous, moss-covered and old, their long, drooping arms heavy with leaves. For the first time since getting out of the train at Swindon, Thorny actually felt cool.

"There's a cement factory in Wychwood Mount?" she asked politely.

"Not yet. Not ever, if we have our way about it." Jenny frowned. "But our dear Squire Belman's not exactly the kind

7

of man to let other people have their way. In the few months since he arrived he's turned the village upside down. Bought Stratton Hall—and where he got the money for that I'll never know. He's not old enough to have earned it." She shrugged. "Probably he inherited it, charming some rich old lady into the ground a few years before her time. He can be charming, if he wants to be. There are a few little fools even here in the village who swoon every time he walks by." She made such a funny face that Thorny grinned. "Anyway, no sooner does he buy the Hall and replace all the servants than he starts applying for planning permission to tear down Awen-Un."

"Awen-Un," Thorny repeated mechanically.

"John never mentioned Awen-Un?" Jenny said indignantly. "That stone circle is the only claim to fame Wychwood Mount has ever had."

Stone circle. Now she remembered. Twelve boulders set up in a ring by people about a zillion years ago. "Yes, Dad did tell me about it," Thorny nodded, "but I've forgotten most of what he said. It's pretty old, though, right?" Thorny had no intention of repeating what Dad had actually said about Awen-Un, not when Aunt Jenny clearly cared about the place.

"Pretty old, indeed! Considering that the stones were dragged here about four thousand years ago by people who didn't even have any decent tools . . . !"

"Is it true no one knows why they did it?"

"It wasn't just for a lark," Jenny said. "You can be sure of that. A dozen four- or five-ton stones, hauled by hand all the way from the downs and then stood upright in a circle—it must have been killing, the work. And now Belman wants to dig up all the stones and cart them off to the rubbish tip! Imagine it, Thorny, tearing down something Stone Age people spent whole lifetimes putting up, just to build a cement factory!"

It did sound awful, put like that. "Does the cement factory have to be built right in that spot?" Thorny asked.

"Belman says it does. Apparently you need chalk to make cement, and supposedly Awen-un stands on top of the best chalk bed in this whole area. Personally, I don't believe it for a minute. I think Belman's just got a thing against everything ancient. If you could just see what he's done to the stand of oaks that used to line the footpath to the church . . . !"

"Can't people stop him?" Thorny asked. "I mean, if Awen-Un's really that old, isn't it against the law for him to tear it down?"

"There is a law protecting ancient monuments in this country," Jenny said gloomily, "but if they've never been listed with the proper government department, and they're on someone's private land, the person who owns the land can do almost anything he wants with them. That's what's happened with Awen-Un. It's one of the oldest stone circles left in Britain, but it never got a lot of attention, not like Stonehenge or Avebury. And it always seemed so safe, sitting on Stratton land, no one bothered to list it. Now it's too late." She rubbed her chin. "We haven't given up, of course. That's what the lunatics are here for. We're all protesting our heads off, hoping the planning board will pay attention and refuse to give Belman permission for the factory. There's a rally on today, actually. You'll be just in time for it, if we hurry." And she pressed her foot down on the gas pedal, while the old car roared.

"When will you know if the planning board's going to let him?" Thorny asked.

"Today, probably." Aunt Jenny sighed. "I'm a bit worried about it. Belman's already taken his case before the board, but the village only just got properly organized a few days ago. And Belman is one of those amazing people who knows exactly what he wants and can somehow always persuade the right people to give it to him."

There was silence in the car. The shaggy, shadowy wood was behind them. The heat descended again, stuffy as a feather pillow and not at all what Thorny had expected of cold, rainy England. They were driving through what seemed to be a park. Grassy areas contrasted with regularly spaced clumps of trees and withering bands of daisies and roses. A narrow stream meandered through the grounds, clearly only a thread of its normal width. There was a cobbled footbridge traversing a little pond that was shallow and scummy with neglect. "One of Belman's little efficiencies," Jenny said dryly, "is not to waste manpower on gardening."

Farther on a curved hedge of yew was the backdrop for a group of statues—perhaps a dozen figures of stone, all different. From the car it was hard to make out what the statues represented, but Thorny was certain she could see a crab and a lion at least, and she thought a fish as well.

"It's a zodiac," her aunt explained. "You know—Leo, Pisces, Gemini, that sort of thing? They were all the rage once, along with man-made lakes, hired hermits and phony grottos. Ghastly, isn't it?" She grinned, her cheerfulness restored.

"Who made the zodiac?" It really was neat, Thorny thought, wishing she could get out of the car and explore it.

"One of the Strattons. It's not terribly old. A century or two, that's all. The stone is decent: nice hard sarsen like at Awen-Un. But that's about all that can be said for it. Patrick likes it, though. He used to spend a lot of time there, B.B. Before Belman," she explained. "Patrick's expression."

"Then Belman owns the zodiac, too?" Thorny was disappointed. Belman didn't sound like the kind of man who'd allow trespassers.

"Belman owns just about everything in Wychwood Mount," Aunt Jenny said. "Everything on both sides of this road, as far as you can see—except Owl Wood back there, and the footpaths, and the public land between them. And, of course, the village proper. If you look over there—" she waved an arm "—you'll see Stratton Hall. He hasn't changed its name yet, but give him time."

Behind the yew hedge a house was coming into view. It was a block of a building with a jutting front like a Greek temple, a top like an astronomical observatory, and at least

10

eight chimneys. A low verandah surmounted by gargoyles and cupids finished off the effect. The Hall was set back some distance from the road. A purplish-coloured hedge separated its grounds from both the road and its nearest neighbour, to which Aunt Jenny was now pointing. "That's our cottage there, on the right. The one just past the Hall."

Jenny's cottage was of stone, small, old, a single grey-stuccoed, rose-rambled storey. It had a thatched roof and diamond-shaped windows of thick leaded glass. The front door was arched, the rich mahogany studded with brass. There were two chimneys, and behind them on the skyline a pair of oak trees and a single weeping willow. The whole area in front of the cottage was garden. Thorny stared, thinking of how her father had described this place. A hole-in-the-wall, he had called it; dingy, small, dark, grim. Could it really have changed so much, since he was young?

Aunt Jenny's cottage had no near neighbour on the side away from Stratton Hall, but across the street there was another small cottage next to a farm building, and farther on, at a bend in the road, an inn. Thorny could just see its sign hanging outside, "The White Horse" hand-lettered beneath a picture of something that looked more like a dragon than a horse.

Then Aunt Jenny turned into the lane of her cottage. "You'll want to change, I expect," she said as she took Thorny's suitcase from the car. "You're just a bit too expensive for a rally."

Thorny nodded, looking with distaste at her Miriam-bought skirt and matching yellow jacket. "Miriam spent a lot of time choosing it," was all her father had said, when over and over again she'd tried to explain why she couldn't stand to wear it. He didn't like it, either, Thorny was sure. Once, a long time ago, he'd told her yellow was awful on her.

"I hope Patrick's all right," Aunt Jenny said over her shoulder, as they went up the walk to her front door. "If the planning board does decide to allow the factory, this rally's apt to turn nasty, and Patrick has a way of getting into the thick of things.''

''You're worried,'' Thorny asked in surprise, ''and you still let him go?'' Miriam wouldn't let you cross the street without a traffic light and a policeman to hold your hand.

''I didn't have much choice,'' Jenny said. ''Patrick's got me rather too well trained. All the same, I'd just as soon be there to keep an eye on him—if you don't mind waiting for your tea, that is.'' She grimaced. ''I have a feeling that it's afterwards that we're all going to need it.''

2
The Circus

"Well, Patrick! Enough excitement for you?"

Mr. Robson, Wychwood Mount's garage mechanic, waved a beefy hand at the throng of people surrounding the stone circle of Awen-Un. It lay just to the east of the public footpath on Belman's land. Awen-Un was not a particularly striking stone circle. It was bigger across than Stonehenge, but its stones were much smaller, and there were only twelve of them. The Keystone was the biggest. This stone, the southernmost in the Circle and the only one with its own name, was less than shoulder height, and even at its broadest could be encompassed by a couple of people with linked hands. The eleven other stones were even stubbier, more like headless turtles than anything else. But they were theirs, Patrick Newport thought loyally. Whatever Belman said about private property, whatever all the outsiders were protesting about, Awen-Un was theirs.

"Did you see the man in the antlers?" Patrick asked Mr. Robson. "Prancing his head off."

"Don't we wish," Mr. Robson said, wiping his forehead with a spotted handkerchief. "Be about as much use at a circus, that one."

It was a bit like a circus, Patrick thought. The milling crowd was everywhere, totally disorganized. There were people picnicking among the stones, people singing, people chatting and marching and waving signs, people looking through magnifying lenses at the stones, even people changing babies' nappies. They were supposed to stay to the west of the public footpath and off Belman's land, but in his absence no one had worried about trespassing.

"Young Peter'll be sorry to miss it all," Mr. Robson went on. "Why anybody'd ever want to spend a summer in Scotland . . .!"

"He had to go," Patrick said loyally. "His whole family was going." Still, it had been a blow. Peter Gordon was Patrick's best friend, the only other boy of Patrick's age in the village.

"Well, at least you'll be having your cousin in from Canada to keep you busy. About your age, right?"

"She's a year younger than me," Patrick said. "And she's a girl."

"Not at all the same." Mr. Robson nodded. "Still, she might be all right, you never know. Treat her like you do my young Jim, why not? He thinks the world of you."

You could hardly point out to Mr. Robson, Patrick told himself, that Thorny might not like being led around on a pony like a four-year-old. Instead he said, "Jim's a good kid. Where is he?"

"At home. No place for a toddler, this isn't. It may be fun and games now, but once Belman shows up, I wouldn't be surprised if things didn't turn nasty. I'd be away myself before then, Patrick, if I was you."

Patrick's blue eyes gleamed. "Yeah, sure," he said innocently. Mr. Robson laughed.

"Should've known better'n to try to warn you off. Never known anything to happen in the village without you being in the thick of it. Better watch out for Belman, though. Whether we like it or not, it is his land." He disappeared into the crowd.

There was a big knot of people at the east end of the Circle, listening to a man give a speech. Patrick wandered towards them. "I've shown you the maps," the man was saying, "and a few of you have checked my compass bearings for yourselves. You've seen with your own eyes that Awen-Un isn't just any stone circle. It's the crossing point of at least

14

a dozen leys, the biggest such centre found anywhere. And this criminal Belman wants to pull it down!''

''What's so blinking important about a ley?'' someone shouted from the back of the crowd. Patrick listened with interest. He didn't know what a ley was, either.

The man at the front sighed, as if this was a question he had already answered a million times. He was a youngish, tweedy fellow with a university accent. But his face was weathered, as if he spent a lot of time outdoors. For one of the lunatics, he seemed quite decent, Patrick thought. ''A ley,'' he answered patiently, ''is a straight line linking various holy places of the past.''

''Don't see any straight lines on this here ground,'' the heckler put in. ''Do you?''

''They're not actually drawn on the ground,'' the speaker replied, still patiently. ''You don't have to see a line to know it's there. Place ten apples in a row, and you call the row a line, right? It's the same with leys. Stone Age people built all their important places—stone circles, single standing stones, tombs, holy wells, tracks—in lines. We call the lines 'leys.' It's my theory that each tribe of people in those days had its own holy line. And that would mean that the place where two or more leys crossed must be especially holy.''

''Because if it was on the crossing point, that put it on both lines?'' Patrick put in, remembering his geometry.

''Right,'' the man said, smiling. ''Being on both lines would mean it was holy to both tribes. That's why Awen-Un is so exciting. It's the crossing point of at least a dozen leys. That means it must have been holy to twelve separate groups of people. If that doesn't make it the most important Stone Age site in England, I don't know what does.''

A new voice came out of the crowd. Patrick recognized the red face and bristly hair of the archaeologist who was staying at the White Horse. Atworthy, his name was. ''Ah, so Jeremy Kingsley finally admits to not knowing something!'' he said, so cold and sneering that Patrick sided with the man called Kingsley at once.

"It was only a manner of speaking," Kingsley replied stiffly. "Anyway, you must agree with me that Awen-Un is important, or you wouldn't be here."

"Important! Of course it's important! It's a perfect example of a Neolithic circle with astronomical alignments. Yet you go on spreading clap-trap—"

"It isn't clap-trap, Atworthy. The lines exist."

"Certainly they do. Not your mythical leys, but real lines of sight, pointing to the midsummer and midwinter sunrise—"

"If we're going to talk astronomy," Kingsley said, "how about the moon? The moon was sacred to Stone Age people long before the sun was. Anyway, just because they were good astronomers, it doesn't mean they couldn't have built ley lines, too."

"You're confusing the issue. To begin with, there is absolutely no evidence of stone circles having sight-lines to the moon. I myself have made a study of the azimuths, and—"

Patrick drifted away. It was all very interesting, he thought, looking at the familiar stone circle with new eyes. All the same, once you let a scientist use a word like "azimuth," you might as well forget about getting any more sense out of him.

The people who had been picnicking among the stones of Awen-Un had finished eating by now. Most of them were drawn to the debate between Kingsley and Atworthy, though a few were following the Morris dancers heading for Lady Copse, a large wood on public land a bit to the southwest of the Circle. There was a wishing-well in the heart of the wood. Patrick supposed that the man with the stag's antlers was going there to dance around it. After all, he had danced around everything else.

A large crowd of demonstrators had begun to march their signs up the footpath towards the crossroads at the centre of the village. Patrick saw Mrs. Millson who kept the post office, and Tom Avery, who normally would have been keeping bar at the White Horse this time of day. Half the village was with them, along with a lot of strangers who normally would

16

never have even known where Wychwood Mount was. They were looking for Belman, obviously. Patrick was tempted to go with them. But if he went back to the village he might see his mother and the new cousin, and get trapped into tea and biscuits.

"Thorny won't want to be here," his mother had warned him, "and I want you to change her mind, no matter how prickly she is." Prickly, sure, with a name like Thorny. And a father like Uncle John . . . Patrick grimaced. He had never met his uncle, but Mum had said enough that Patrick had a pretty good picture of him. Mr. Successful himself. Practically ran Toronto, it sounded like. Thorny was probably a snobby little city girl who'd turn her nose up at shabby carpets and sleeping on a sofa bed. Patrick turned decisively away from the marching crowd. If he only had a few hours of freedom left, he'd spend it here in the Circle. He wandered towards the Keystone.

There was a man in the Circle, quite alone. He was as tall as Mr. Robson, but a lot thinner, with a shock of white hair. His tanned face was lined and sharp-nosed, like a hawk, Patrick thought, or maybe an owl. The man was walking slowly across the Circle, sometimes stopping and retracing his steps or dropping the stick he carried to write in his notebook, sometimes consulting the compass slung around his neck, moving first sideways, then straight ahead. It took a few moments for Patrick to realize that though his path was indirect, he was making steadily for the Keystone. He wasn't even looking at it, but he was heading for it as certainly as if it drew him.

The stick the man held was forked—hazel, Patrick guessed from of the looks of it. He held one fork in each hand, and his knuckles were white. Patrick drew closer. The hazel twig was twisting in the man's grip, so hard that the green bark was being stripped off. It really looked as if it were twisting by itself and the man was trying to stop it. Beads of sweat were dripping into his white eyebrows.

At last, at the foot of the Keystone, the twig seemed to leap from the man's hands. It fell to the ground, and the man grunted, blowing on his fingers. Reaching into his pocket, he added a squiggle to a page and put it away again. It was only then that he looked at Patrick. "I suppose," he said gruffly, "you want to know what I'm doing."

"I think I know," Patrick said. "You were dowsing, weren't you? Talbots' had a dowser once when their well dried up. He found an underground spring with a forked stick just like yours. The end of the stick went down all by itself, he said, when he was directly over the spring. He wouldn't let me watch him doing it, though."

"But you tried dowsing anyway, I suppose?"

"Yes. It didn't work, though. The stick never budged. I must've been doing it wrong. How did you know I'd tried?" he added.

"You look like the sort of boy who would."

A bit aggressively Patrick said, "Well, you can't dig a well here. This isn't public land, and anyway, Belman wants to tear this whole place down to quarry for chalk. I'm surprised you don't know."

"Belman won't get any chalk here," the man said with a rather grim smile. "As soon as he sticks his shovel in, he'll be lucky if he doesn't drown."

"Did Belman hire you to find that out?"

The dowser gave a short laugh. "Not likely!"

"But there is water here." Patrick thought over the implications of this. "I get it," he said suddenly. "You were doing it on your own, hoping you'd find out his factory was going to flood. So now all you have to do is tell him, and he won't build—" He broke off, seeing the dowser's face. "I suppose he'd have to believe you first," he muttered. "I mean, to him you might be just another lun—that is, not everyone believes in dowsing."

"No, not everyone does. You believe in it, though, even though you couldn't do it. Now I wonder why that is?"

"I saw you with that stick. You weren't moving it by yourself."

"You'd be amazed what people can see with their own eyes and not believe. If this Belman of yours is an ordinary businessman, he'll believe what he wants, regardless of what I or anybody else could tell him about underground water. And if he isn't—"

Patrick stared. "If he isn't a businessman? But why else would he be trying to build a cement works?"

The man shrugged. There was a dismissing look in his eyes, as if he'd judged Patrick and found him to be not very useful. "Utterly senseless, of course," he said flatly. "Now, if you'll excuse me—" He started to turn away.

"He doesn't like old things," Patrick said quickly. "He cut down a lot of really ancient oak trees, and Awen-Un's much older than they were. You don't suppose . . . ?" The dowser was regarding him with interest, but Patrick wound down, thinking aloud. "No, this is different. To go to all this trouble, trying to get planning permission, getting the whole village worked up. And it's going to cost the earth to get those stones out. Belman would have to be mad, to do it just because old things get on his nerves."

"And he isn't mad, I suppose?" The dowser really seemed to want to know.

"No," Patrick said slowly. "He's not exactly what I'd call normal, but . . . . Haven't you seen him?"

"I don't believe so. Not . . . lately."

"Belman's smooth," Patrick went on. "So smooth you could slip on him. Mum says it comes from always getting his own way. He acts like he's the only adult in the village and the rest of us are just a bunch of babies. You wouldn't believe it, but some people like being treated like that. Girls, mostly," he shrugged. "You know what they are."

The dowser didn't even smile. He bent to pick up his dowsing stick.

"I don't get it," Patrick said. "Why were you dowsing, if you never intended to tell Belman about the water here?"

"I wasn't actually looking for water," the man said.

"But I thought—"

"There are other things underground besides springs." The man hesitated for a moment. "We dowsers call them earth-forces. They're currents, like streams of electricity underground, everywhere on earth, actually. Have you never wondered why cattle always take the same path, day after day; and deer in the wild? They sense the forces, you see, and that's where they walk. Dowsers can feel them through their forked sticks in the same way they sense the presence of underground streams."

"I wish I knew what it felt like," Patrick said enviously.

"You and a lot of other people," the man said. "The ones who don't think we're mad, that is." He flexed his fingers, then placed them around the dowsing stick in a businesslike way.

"So were you trying to find the lines of force here at Awen-Un?" Patrick remembered the compass and the squiggles in the notebook. "You were mapping them, weren't you?"

The man nodded. "Each stone circle has its own pattern of forces, you see. And Awen-Un being in danger of destruction, you might say I was merely trying to map its pattern before it's lost forever." He shrugged. "Look here, boy, whatever your name is—"

"Patrick. Patrick Newport."

"Right, then. Look, Patrick. I have at least two more hours' work to do here, and only about an hour to do it in."

As hints went, it was fairly broad. "Can't I help?" Patrick asked hopefully. "I could write things down while you dowse. That'd save time. Or I could hold things. I'd like to help, really."

Again that faint smile warmed the man's face. "It's not always as simple as it seems, helping. You might find yourself doing more than you expect."

"I don't mind." Patrick was quite startled at his own eagerness.

The man looked at him, so long and so deep that Patrick almost blushed. Suddenly he seemed to make up his mind. "Right," he said briskly, handing him his notebook and pencil. "I'll call out the compass bearings and distances, and you write them down. Oh, by the way, my name's Underwood. Alec, to you. If we're going to be working together, you have to know what to call me."

3

A Very Dangerous Man

Thorny's bedroom was at the side of the cottage, near the back. It was a small room with rose-patterned walls, a couch that pulled out into a bed, and a single chest of drawers with a mirror. A sewing machine stood on a table by the window, a pile of clothes beside it. "The mending has to block the window completely before I can force myself to sew," Aunt Jenny said cheerfully. "Need some help unpacking?"

Thorny shook her head. "I didn't bring much. Just tops and jeans." Jeans she'd salvaged from the pile Miriam had been collecting for the Salvation Army. There hadn't been anything wrong with them, either.

"That's all you'll need. And I've given you lots of drawer-space. This chest is almost empty—" Jenny pulled out the top drawer, and her voice broke off. "Gracious! Now where do you suppose this came from?"

Thorny went over to look. Inside the drawer was a bouquet. It was a perfect little thing, neatly gathered and shaped, though there seemed to be nothing holding the stems together. It was mostly leaves, but they were beautiful, deeply lobed and a rich, dark, shiny green. Scattered throughout the leaves were small white flowers with a faint scent. Wonderingly, Thorny lifted the bouquet out of the drawer. "Mind the prickles," her aunt warned, but Thorny didn't hear. The bouquet fit her hands as if it had been made for them. She buried her face in the leaves, sniffing.

"It doesn't really smell," Aunt Jenny said.

But it did, Thorny thought. The more you sniffed at it, the more you noticed it. It smelled of everything that was green and wild and alive.

"What kind of plant is it?" she asked.

Her aunt smiled. "Haven't you ever seen the tree you're named for?"

"You mean it's hawthorn? But it can't be. It's so pretty."

"Did you think it'd be ugly? Why? Because it has thorns? A rose has thorns, but no one could call it ugly."

"It's not that. I just thought . . . well, hawthorn's supposed to be unlucky . . ."

"Good grief, where did you hear that?"

Thorny was quiet for a moment, remembering. It had been a joke, that was all, just another of Dad's stories, like the one about her being born on a Friday the thirteenth after her mother had walked under a ladder, silly stuff like that. But if it was really true that hawthorn was unlucky, and Dad knew it when he named her, didn't that mean something not very nice? That was why she'd looked it up, wanting to prove to herself that Dad had only been teasing.

"I read about it in an encyclopedia," she told her aunt. "It said hawthorn was the favourite tree of witches. I don't care," she added quickly. "Things like that don't bother me."

Aunt Jenny looked at her sharply. After a moment she said, "Witchcraft wasn't always totally evil, you know, Thorny. Long before the birth of Christianity, the word 'witch' used to be 'wicca,' which meant 'wise one.' It was a religion, a good one in its way, treating the earth with respect, understanding the role of man in nature. A great many of the things that were sacred to that old religion were carried over into witchcraft, when it developed. Hawthorn may have been one." Thorny looked unconvinced. "Anyway," Jenny said firmly, "it's a pretty name, and that may have been all that mattered when your parents were looking for a name for you. From all the pictures your mother sent me, you were a very pretty baby."

"My mother sent you pictures?" Thorny said in amazement.

"Dozens. Every time she wrote. Do you want to see them?"

"No," she said hastily. Her mother had sent pictures. Just like any mother, proud of her baby. And eight years afterwards she was gone. She had wanted a life of her own, Dad had explained when Thorny finally managed to ask. A life of her own. Yet every now and then a letter came from her, or an invitation for Thorny; never when they should, never when Thorny needed them—and yet they came. Thorny looked down, her fingers tightening around the bouquet in her hands.

"We seem to have gone a long way from your little bouquet," Aunt Jenny said at last. "And quite a little mystery it is, too. I wonder how it got here."

Thorny blinked. "Didn't you put it there?"

"I'm as surprised by it as you. I suppose it must have been Patrick," she said slowly. "Only he and I have keys to the cottage. But it's not at all like him. He used to pick me flowers, but they always ended up looking as if they'd been run over by a bus. Not like this." And she indicated the perfection of the arrangement, still as fresh as if it were growing on the tree. "Besides, he hasn't given me flowers for years. You know boys when they get past age ten!"

Thorny, who didn't, could only nod.

"I'll put this in water for you," Aunt Jenny said, gingerly taking the bouquet out of Thorny's hands. "It was thoughtful of Patrick, I must say. A very personal welcome . . ." But her voice as she went out the door was still decidedly puzzled.

Thorny finished unpacking, threw on a pair of jeans and a shirt, and ran her hands through her hair. She found Aunt Jenny in the front room, staring intently out of the window towards the street. "Come and get your first view of Awen-Un's nemesis, Thorny," she said, gripping the net curtain tightly.

There was a man on horseback out on the street. His back was to them, but just from the way he sat on the horse, Thorny guessed he was a man used to command. He had wavy reddish hair, long enough that each lock seemed separate, taking on a life of its own. He held a riding crop in one hand, but loosely, almost absently. The other held the reins of his horse. It was a black mare, rigid with immobility. Thorny didn't ride, but there was something wrong about that horse, she knew it. It was trying too hard, being too obedient. It wasn't normal.

"Is that Belman?" Thorny asked.

"In the flesh," Aunt Jenny nodded.

There were a lot of men in a crowd in front of Belman. They carried ropes and crowbars and picks, and looked pretty tough. Belman was talking to them, giving them orders, it looked like. But still he was relaxed, the hand holding the riding crop resting comfortably on the saddle. Thorny kept having to make herself look away from it. "Are those men from the village?" she asked, turning to her aunt.

"No. They're a bad lot, I should say, but good enough for dirty work, and that's what needs doing." Aunt Jenny tried to smile. "I saw the crane go by a few minutes ago. The planning board must have given in."

Thorny was silent. After a moment she said, "Isn't there anything people can do?"

"We could appeal," Jenny said. "But by that time there isn't going to be much left of Awen-Un to fight over. Belman's got everything organized. Winches and cables and a crane for the stones, an all-terrain vehicle to get the crane over to the Circle, all those cutthroats to do the hard work, and policemen in from outside to protect them with the strong arm of the law. Blast Belman, anyway!"

Just then the labourers began to move away from Belman, determinedly heading down the street. "I'll bet he's promised them all jobs in the factory when it's built," Aunt Jenny said. "There's a lot of unemployment in Swindon lately."

"Isn't Belman going to the Circle with them?" Thorny asked.

It was almost as if he had heard her. Slowly, deliberately, his head swivelled, turning to look in her direction. Thorny drew back in sudden fright. Then, half against her will, she pressed forward again so that she could see his face. It was a bold, dominating face, the cheekbones wide and high, casting their own shadow. In that shadow the edges of his mouth were strange, neither smiling nor frowning yet somehow seeming to do both at once, while the central part, the flaring upper lip and the full, secret lower one, merely waited. His brows were absolutely straight, meeting and combining over his nose so that they seemed one long slash. His eyes were alive, black and warm, seeking her out. Thorny shivered at the heat that seemed to come from them.

"That," Aunt Jenny said deliberately, "is a very dangerous man."

And Belman, sweeping a low, suave bow to the two faces in the window, touched his riding crop to the neck of his horse. It was the lightest of touches, more a caress than a command, but the horse leapt forward as if galvanized. With an angry flick of the wrist Aunt Jenny let the curtain drop back down.

"Come on, Thorny," she said. "Let's go. Or it'll all be over before we get there."

4

The Keystone

Three o'clock. In the Circle the sun beat down. Patrick felt breathless, his fingers slipping on the pencil Alec had given him, sweat trickling down his neck. Alec was calling out the numbers more quickly now, no longer explaining anything, no longer even friendly. Something was going to happen, Patrick knew it.

He was leaning against the Keystone, using it as a prop while he wrote. Suddenly the stone seemed to shiver. Patrick's heart jumped. A lot of people shouted at once. And then, at the top of the rise where the footpath overlooked the Circle, he saw the crane.

It was an ungainly thing, towed at the back of a land-rover, jangling and swaying on the bumpy footpath, its steel shaft blinding in the sunlight. Slowly, unstoppably, it headed for Awen-Un, surrounded by the mob of angry demonstrators. There were police there, too, perhaps a dozen uniformed men making a not too complete ring around the vehicle to keep the crowd off. Patrick whistled under his breath. So Belman had won, after all. He'd got his stinking permission, and wasn't even waiting a day to put it into effect.

"Damn!" he muttered. "Damn, damn, damn."

Alec looked over his shoulder quickly. "X to Y, distance three feet, angle 17 degrees," he repeated sharply.

"But Belman—"

27

"—will be starting on the Keystone," Alec cut in. "We've got to finish mapping the forces now, or we never will. Get me?"

Patrick wrote the numbers down. But what good would they be, once the stones were gone? He looked up, seeing a sign come crashing into a windshield of the rover. For a brief moment he felt savage with satisfaction.

"Patrick!" Alec demanded, and he turned back to the notebook with a shock.

"Four point five, eighty," he hurriedly repeated Alec's next set of numbers, then stole a quick look at the footpath while Alec did some measuring. The crane was still on the footpath directly opposite the Circle. It had stopped, and the crowd took heart from this, yelling at the police who defended it. No one was looking back. No one but Patrick. He alone saw Belman arrive. The red-haired man reined in at the top of the rise, looking calmly down on the mob below. He laid a hand on his horse's neck, and the horse was still. Behind Patrick's back Alec said something, and Patrick's attention jerked away.

"Two feet, two twenty-five degrees," he repeated mechanically. Then, "Four, two seventy. Two, seventeen. Are we finished?"

"Near enough," Alec said, with a quick movement sliding the compass into the neck of his shirt. "And we're out of time, it looks like."

They were alone in the Circle. Belman was still up on the rise, but he wasn't looking at the mob anymore, he was looking at them. Patrick could feel those dark eyes weighing them, wondering. Patrick tried to make himself stare back, but he couldn't. He looked at Alec, instead, who was casually breaking his dowsing stick into pieces.

"Hey, why're you—?" he began, but Alec gave him a look, and he stopped.

Now Belman was riding down the footpath and into the crowd, which became aware of him for the first time. Red faces turned his way, and fists were shaken.

"Bloody nob!" someone shouted. "Take away our heritage, would you?"

"Tinpot dictator! Thinks 'e owns the world!" bellowed someone else.

Belman ignored the crowd, speaking only to a rotund, sweating body in police uniform. "Sergeant Quigley," he said politely, his warm, rich voice carrying through the sudden silence. "I'm a little worried about people getting hurt while we're setting up the machinery. If you could just clear everybody back to the public side of the footpath . . ."

"Clear *him* off, Mr. Sergeant," somebody jeered.

"Yeah! Go after the real lawbreakers, why don't you?"

"Put him away!" Aggie Millson shrilled. "Destruction of property. Public nuisance."

"Now then, now then," the harassed Sergeant Quigley said nervously. "Back to the path, all of you. We don't want any trouble."

Suddenly a group of big, powerful-looking men appeared at the top of the rise overlooking the Circle. They carried crowbars, ropes and picks, and were heading purposefully for the rover.

"Watch out!" warned one of the protestors, and people began to fall back. Not fast enough, though. A woman screamed as one of the newcomers jabbed her husband with a crowbar. What had been a family picnic was fast turning nasty, and a lot of the people who'd come to Wychwood Mount from outside quickly withdrew, heading for the village and the safety of their cars. Even the villagers retreated, but only as far as the footpath, where they gathered in a tight knot. From here the solid bulk of Mr. Robson stepped forward.

"Had to go foreign for that lot, did you, Belman?" he said. "And the police, too. Funny what money will buy these days!" Sergeant Quigley flushed angrily, but Belman simply urged his horse forward towards the crane. He reined in beside the rover and nodded to the driver, a bald-headed man whom Patrick had seen working around the Hall.

"Everything under control, Red?" Without waiting for an answer he jerked his head at the workers. "Start on the southernmost stone," Belman said in an easy drawl that everyone could hear. "That one over there. The one they call the Keystone."

The ley-hunter called Kingsley stepped out of the crowd. "In the name of God, Belman, don't do this! It's only chalk! You can get it anywhere! Why destroy something thousands of years old for—?"

Atworthy the archaeologist joined him, for once his ally. "At least can't you wait until the scientists have had a chance to—?"

"The scientists have had centuries to do what they wanted here," Belman replied. "I have the planning board's decision in black and white. That is all that should concern you." He turned away.

Atworthy reddened, but Jeremy Kingsley was angrier still. "I warn you, Belman," he called, "you'll live to regret this! Stones have their own ways of getting even."

Belman paused, then faced him. "Are you threatening me?" he asked pleasantly.

"Call it a warning," Kingsley returned. "These old stones don't like to be moved. People who try it often find they wish they hadn't."

"I'll take my chances," Belman smiled as he touched his crop to the mare's neck. "There are two people still in the Circle," he added to Sergeant Quigley, as the horse moved forward.

30

Patrick looked at Alec, who was standing very still, his eyes unreadable. Belman pulled up just outside the Circle, staring at Alec and Patrick. He said nothing, but under his look Patrick twitched nervously.

"All right, we're going," Alec said. He put his hand on Patrick's shoulder. "Come on, Patrick." And under Belman's steady, thoughtful gaze, they marched out of the Circle.

Through the burning afternoon Thorny followed her aunt along the path towards the Circle, her thoughts buzzing. Whatever Aunt Jenny said, she didn't really believe that Patrick had provided the hawthorn bouquet. Who, then? And why? It made Thorny feel slightly sick to think that someone had crept into Jenny's cottage and hidden the bouquet in the room that would be Thorny's, knowing she would be sleeping there, knowing her real name. Unless it was all just a coincidence and the hawthorn hadn't been meant for her after all. Sure, Thorny thought. Someone got mixed up and broke into Aunt Jenny's locked cottage by mistake, and then quite naturally hid the bouquet in a bureau drawer in a sewing room. No, it was all just too crazy. It must have been Patrick after all.

It was a rolling, grassy landscape, empty even of trees. The nearest wood was Lady Copse, but it was out of sight behind a hill, as was the Circle itself. Thorny and Jenny climbed the hill in silence, following the footpath, cloudy now from the passage of so many people. The sky was a blaze of blue. Thorny felt breathless, like a fish caught and strung to dry.

"There," Aunt Jenny said at last. Thorny stopped and stared.

Far away to the east and south she saw the main road, like a dusty ribbon winding over the parched downs, dipping under the railway tunnel where the reporter had parked, then heading north for the village crossroads. Thorny followed it as far as she could see, past the cool green of Owl Wood with the church spire in the foreground, past Stratton Park, right up to the jutting opulence of the Hall. From there she looked westward across all the land that was Belman's to the defiant green of Lady Copse, on the public side of the footpath. It was larger than Owl Wood, and even in the dazzling sunlight looked cool and dark. Finally, almost reluctantly, she looked at Awen-Un, just to the left of the footpath.

It was a small ring of stones, twelve grey humps standing in a circle. They looked perfectly ordinary, just like the thousand others that littered the downs. Except that they weren't ordinary. They caught her gaze and held it, and it was like drowning.

"Blast the man," Aunt Jenny said. "He would start on the Keystone."

She was pointing at the southernmost stone. Thorny's fingernails curled into her palms as she watched the men wrapping it with chains and digging at it, forcing crowbars into the earth beneath. A mechanical crane was waiting for the chains to be hooked to it. Belman, still mounted, was overseeing things silently. On the footpath and beyond, a lot of other people were watching, too. Signs waving and fists shaking, they shouted and jostled one another and buzzed, held back by a line of policemen. The Keystone was striped with black marks where the greasy chains had scraped it. It made Thorny sick to look at it.

"I can't see Patrick," Jenny said, her voice anxious.

Thorny shook herself. "Sorry?" she asked her aunt.

"Patrick," Jenny repeated, straining her eyes. "I can't spot him."

"What does he look like?"

"Your height. Dark hair, tanned, blue eyes." She took her niece's arm, and they began to hurry down the slope towards the massed crowd. "He'll be wearing—oh, hullo, Gladys. You haven't seen Patrick, have you?" They had reached the outer line of people. A dozen other strangers surrounded them, hemming them in.

"T'other side, Jen. Leastways, he was. Belman picked him out proper. He's with an outsider. Tall chap with white hair."

Jenny nodded her thanks and pushed her way forward into the jam. Thorny tried to follow. "Excuse me," she said, but the woman called Gladys was in the way. Four Morris dancers shoved their way between Thorny and the woman, saying something about there being no law against making music. The crowd shifted, and Thorny was alone.

5

The Lady in White

There was no sign of Aunt Jenny. Even Jenny's friend Gladys was gone. Thorny could just barely make out a pair of stag's antlers waving over the bobbing heads, but otherwise she recognized no one at all. It was an unpleasant feeling, being totally alone in a strange place, hovering on the edge of an angry, threatening mob. She hesitated, wondering what to do. And as she hesitated she became aware that there was someone behind her, watching her.

She turned. A short distance away a solitary woman stood quietly. It was her eyes that Thorny noticed first: blue dispassionate eyes, deep as the sky, cold as a mountain pool, electric as St. Elmo's fire. They held Thorny's gaze as securely as a mother holds a child. Mesmerized, Thorny stared into their depths, drowning in them. Then, with a wrench, she tore her attention away.

The woman was still silent, still watching her. Her long, gauzy dress might have seemed odd anywhere else, but in the motley crowd at the rally it didn't stand out. The only thing that made it different from all the others was its colourlessness: white as a new sheet, with pale shadows decorating its folds. She wore the dress regally, like a queen's nightgown, Thorny thought. Its only adornment was a silver belt like a chain of leaves. Her features were sharp and beautiful, and her skin was white: a night person's white, untouched by the sun.

Again Thorny saw her eyes, and again she looked away, though more than ever they were compelling, like glittering blue stones in a white desert. The lady smiled then, red lips parted wide. Her hair hung thick and long down her back, its colour that rare blond that is almost white, with no hint of gold in it at all. There were leaves in it, green and shiny and pricked with thorns. With a chill Thorny knew that they were hawthorn.

"Thou art Hawthorn," the lady said, her voice pale and bright, like moonlight on shadow. Thorny shivered at its beauty. At her back the crowd muttered and rumbled. Farther away Belman's men heaved on the Keystone. Farther still, Belman's head turned, searching the crowd for something he couldn't see. But for all the activity and noise, Thorny and the lady in white might have been alone.

"Thou art Hawthorn," the woman repeated, clear and sure.

Thorny frowned. *Thou art?* And how did she know Thorny's name?

"I know thee," the woman said. "Thine age is three and nine of the sun's years. Thy birth was in the month thou callest August, under the harvest full moon. Father and mother hadst thou then, and love. Now no mother hast thou, nor any love but mine."

Thorny flushed angrily. "Who do you think you are, talking to me like this? I may just be twelve, if that's what you mean by three and nine, but I'm old enough to—and, anyway, how come you know so much about me? Did Aunt Jenny tell you?" But even as she spoke she knew it couldn't be true. Plainly this lady was no villager, and Aunt Jenny would never have told a stranger about her. Especially not anything about her mother.

"Thou art known to me," the woman said gently. "Thou art hawthorn in more than name. Like it, thou art strongest

35

when thou strugglest. Like it, thou hast a thorn. And like it, most like, thou art beloved of the Goddess.''

Goddess? Did she really mean herself? Thorny swallowed. The woman was crazy as a loon. Quickly she looked over her shoulder, but there was no one near enough to help.

"I am not mad," the lady said tranquilly. "If I were mad, how would I know so much about thee?" She smiled, still so gentle that Thorny had to fight to retain her anger and fear. "Does it not please thee, Hawthorn, to know that I love thee?"

"I don't even know you!"

"Doest thou not? Thou hast dreamed me, child, many times."

Thorny stared at her, vague memories whispering in her mind. There *had* been dreams with a woman in them. She had been beautiful and kind. The dreams had come on birthdays, Christmas, the day Thorny acted in her class play, the time she had had her tonsils out—all the times her mother had not been there. She swallowed. "I don't believe you. I don't care what you know about me. I don't believe you!"

"Thou doest, Hawthorn." She touched the hawthorn in her hair, so soft, so loving, it made Thorny want to scream.

"You're the one who left that bouquet in my room, weren't you?" she demanded.

"Thy namesake," the lady nodded. "To welcome thee."

"So breaking and entering is another one of your talents? Is that how you know so much about me? Because you've been reading other people's mail, listening in on private conversations? Well, let me tell you—"

"I need none of thy words, nor any other's, to tell me what thou art!" Now the lady was hard and cold as winter steel. "I was there at thy birth. I saw thy father name thee Hawthorn, child of ill luck. I saw him frown."

36

Thorny's eyes blazed. "You're lying! Dad wanted me, he did! It was Mum who—"

"He wants thee now, yes, as he wanted thy mother, as he wants this other woman who is now his wife. He wants thy devotion. There are those who need the worship of others. He is not the only one."

"What do you want from me? Who are you?" Thorny whispered, backing away. She was shaking. It was horrible to hear a stranger say these things.

"Thou askest my name? Rather ask the moon's name, or the earth's, or the darkest grave's." Her voice had changed, turning deep and merciless. 'I am She who was First. I am Three and I am Nine. Seek not to learn my name, rather seek to know why thou hast been brought here. There is a world beneath this one, Hawthorn, a world that is the foundation of the one thou knowest. It is for that world that thou wert created."

"I don't know what you're talking about," Thorny said desperately. "Anyway, I've got to find Aunt Jenny." She tried to turn away, but her muscles wouldn't obey.

"I cannot command thee," the lady said. "Not in the great things, not in the thing that is needed. I no longer have that power over humans. Long ago I would not have sought mortal help, nor counted any human mine enemy, but now is not then. Now mine ancient enemy cloaks himself as one of thee, and fights me in thy garb. The moon grows nightly, yet each night my power wanes. Stones tremble in their sockets and the green world withers and burns. It is unnatural, against all pattern. It hath the stink of chaos. Wilt thou walk away, Hawthorn, with thy world in pieces? Wilt thou risk a moon shining alone in an empty sky?"

Thorny's lips trembled. She wanted to walk away. But she couldn't. Mutely she shook her head. No matter what, she wouldn't believe a thing this woman said.

"In time thou wilt believe," the lady said. "Mine enemy tries to destroy me, but he will not. He will destroy only my domain here on Earth. But to thee that will be everything. In this thy world the green will die and the ground will be rent with fire and flood. Pattern will unravel and order will be lost. Wilt thou watch as thy world dies? Or wilt thou stop him?"

"But how can I—?" Thorny broke off. "Look, I'm just a kid. You say you're a . . . and anyway, if *you* can't stop him—"

"We are inaccessible to each other while he remains in human form. And he is on guard against me. But he will not be on guard against thee. That makes him vulnerable. Thou wilt know his weakness, when the time comes."

"Look, whoever you are—"

"Look for thyself! Look at my Circle! It is Awen-Un, the first, the mother of all circles, the centre of control. At another time I could have protected it, and the world with it. Even now, for a few more days, I will keep it safe. But three days hence, when the moon will be devoured, it will be all I can do to preserve myself." She raised her hand, white and commanding and terrible. "Do not speak. Listen! Remember! The Keystone will be removed, yet it will return. Twice will this happen. And after the second time thou wilt see the full moon rise only to be eaten by darkness. Thou wilt hear the stones scream. Thou wilt watch pattern unravel into chaos. Then must thou act, lest thou wouldst know a world gone mad."

"Act how? What do you want me to—?"

"Save Awen-Un."

"But—"

A hand came out from behind and gripped her elbow. Thorny whirled, wild-eyed and distraught. But it was only a boy, rather short and stocky, with a stubborn-looking jaw.

"I'm Patrick," he said. He jerked his head towards the footpath where Jenny was gesturing extravagantly to someone. "Mum's in a flap. We're going home." He eyed her soberly. "You always talk to thin air?"

Thorny blinked at him. Thin air. Desperately she looked back over her shoulder. The lady in white was gone.

"There was someone here with me," she said, turning back to Patrick. "A lady. All in white. We were talking. You must have seen her."

"No," said Patrick.

"But you must have! She couldn't have—"

"No." He gave her a searching look.

Thorny took a grip on herself. "She must have slipped off," she muttered. "Into the crowd, I mean . . ."

Patrick's brows rose. There wasn't any crowd here. The people had moved on down the footpath. Did Thorny daydream like this all the time? Or was she just trying to make herself interesting?

The noise of the crowd rose suddenly to a roar. "The Keystone! It's out!"

Beneath the yells of dismay, the cheers of the workmen, the shouted commands from the police, was another sound: a groaning cry, deep and sick and faint, like something dying. Not everyone heard it, but Thorny and Patrick did. Apprehensively they looked at each other, seeing their own awareness mirrored in the other's eyes. "What is it?" Patrick mouthed, his voice lost in the uproar. Thorny shook her head, glad she didn't have to answer. *Thou wilt hear the stones scream.* No. It couldn't be.

Together, determinedly, they went forward into the crowd, making their way to the front. They stood there then, watching the Keystone rising from its socket. Slowly it rose— heavy, awkward, a great lumbering thing with no dignity left. Finally it cleared the ground, while the men heaved and sweated and the crane almost seemed to bend. The shouts of the crowd faded, dying to nothing. At last only the creak and groan of the Keystone was left, dangling on its chain like a corpse on a gibbet. In front of it Belman sat silent, his horse trembling beneath him. No one could see his face.

"This is awful," Patrick muttered finally, feeling as if he were witnessing a murder. "Let's get out of here." He didn't look at Thorny, nor she at him. They made their way back to Jenny. Quietly, almost ashamedly, the three of them headed back to the cottage. And behind them, creaking and rattling, the Keystone of Awen-Un was taken away.

6

After Midnight

It was after ten when Thorny got to bed that night, but in spite of her long day she couldn't sleep. She lay in bed looking for moonlight through the leaves outside her window, trying not to think. It was amazingly dark. Thorny had known that people went to bed early in the country, but she had not been prepared for the intense blackness that descended when all man-made lights were turned off. Even the moon seemed dim and far away, though it was high in the sky and almost full.

It was a restless night, windy and hot. Everything small and light and quiet was in motion: fallen bits of branches, gauzy curtains, puffs of dust, willow leaves. The noise they made was tiny, but it scratched like a cat at the back of Thorny's mind. Outside a dog barked twice. Then the night returned to its whispers.

Thorny thought of Toronto whose noise was so different, loud and easy to ignore; as at the wedding on Saturday, with the intermittent roar from the nearby airport drowning out organ and vows alike. The church had been modern and expensive-looking: John McCall's choice, though he had never been in it until they began planning the wedding. Miriam had suggested her own church, an old, beautiful chapel near the university, but John had said it was too small. She had wanted to wear a white gown, too, but John had said something amused about old-fashioned girls, and that was the end of that. Miriam worshipped John. It was the only thing about her that Thorny could understand.

Until Miriam, there had only been Dad and Thorny. It had been Thorny who put Mrs. Cornell's casserole in the oven, waiting dinner until John could get home, sometimes not until nine o'clock at night. It had been Thorny to whom John talked at meals, stuff about banking and the economy and wild-headed fools in the government, things she didn't understand, though she tried to. Once he had taken her on holiday to New York, a whole wonderful week to celebrate her ninth birthday. He'd treated her like a grownup, opening doors for her, taking her to plays and dining out afterwards, buying her violets on street corners, talking to her about art. She hadn't minded not understanding most of it. And she had hardly once thought about the fact that this was the week her mother had invited her to visit, the first time since the separation.

There are those who need the worship of others . . . . Angrily Thorny made a ball of the sheet in her hands. What was the matter with her? As if Dad would be nice to her only so she wouldn't think about Mum!

In bed Thorny turned over, listening to the wind. It was getting stronger, tossing the branches on the tree outside, sending old leaves scuttering. Away over in Wychwood St. Stephen's Church a bell clanged, faint and mournful; nothing like the glorious hymn the bells had rung after Evensong that night. Patrick and Jenny had taken Thorny to the service. Thorny wasn't used to going to church on a Tuesday, but to her surprise most of the village was there.

Afterwards Aunt Jenny and Thorny had waited for Patrick, who was a bellringer. They had sat on a bench in the church-yard. Jenny was immersed in the newspaper, looking for an announcement of that day's planning committee's meeting.

42

She wanted to find a list of the members, she told Thorny, so she could write and tell them what she thought of them. The sun was going down but its heat remained, squeezing like an olive-press. Thorny had thought of the Keystone, glistening with grease like a kind of sweat. And then Aunt Jenny had looked up from her paper.

"Here's something interesting," she had said. "Patrick will have to get out his telescope. There's going to be an eclipse of the moon on Friday."

"An eclipse?" Thorny's throat was dry.

Her aunt thought she didn't understand the word. "They call it an eclipse," she had explained, "when the earth, the moon and the sun all line up. This time the earth is going to be in the middle, so it'll cast a gigantic shadow over the moon. It's an eerie sight, seeing the moon go from full to nothing in just a couple of hours." She smiled. "I remember my first time. I was just a little thing, and I got quite panicky, thinking the moon was being eaten up by the dark."

Thorny was silent. *Three days hence, when the moon will be devoured. . . . Thou wilt see the full moon rise only to be eaten by darkness.* Three days from now was Friday, when the paper said the eclipse would take place.

In bed, remembering the whole thing, Thorny shook her head violently. It was a coincidence, that was all. The lady in white had heard about the eclipse somewhere, and made it part of her act. Anyway, it didn't make her other statements any less crazy. The Keystone returning—not once, but twice. Stones screaming. A world gone mad. . . . Thorny punched her pillow violently. It was all crazy. She threw back her sheet and got out of bed. She needed some air.

Somewhere in the cottage a clock chimed twelve. Thorny padded over to the window. Outside the wind was crying; low, sighing wails that set the hair on Thorny's neck on end. The trees in the garden were swaying in sympathy, flickering in the cloud-scattered moonlight like a scene in an old movie. Thorny leaned against the window, shuddering in the cold air that swirled against her body. What had happened to the heat? Somewhere a dog began barking, loud and frantic. Another dog joined in, and another. Close to the cottage a cat yowled. The wind smelled of cold, wet earth.

Suddenly Thorny was afraid. Her hands felt rubbery and icy cold, but somehow she got the window shut and herself back into bed. It was a long time before she fell asleep.

"Don't bother making your bed," Patrick said from the doorway. "It's Mrs. Hill's day, and she always changes the sheets. Gosh, it's hot in here! Do you always sleep with your window shut?"

Thorny looked up from the pillow she was fluffing. "It got cold last night," she said shortly.

"Well, it's not now. It's hot enough outside to sizzle bacon. Which reminds me. Mum wants to know what you eat for breakfast."

"I hope she's not cooking specially for me. I'm not really very hungry."

"I didn't think you would be. Only the English know how to eat breakfast."

"Dad's English," Thorny said, "and he just has coffee."

"Your father doesn't count. He hates England, doesn't he? Funny, him feeling like that and still wanting you to stay here all summer. Did you do something to annoy him, or what?"

Thorny was silent. That was something she had been trying not to wonder about. Of course she had to go somewhere while Dad and Miriam were on their honeymoon. Mrs. Cornell had already told them she'd be going to help her daughter with the new baby, and Thorny couldn't have stayed home alone. But she could have gone to her friend Anne's. Or maybe . . . maybe she could have accepted the latest of her mother's invitations and stayed with her. She had mentioned both ideas to her father, but a few days later he told her he'd arranged for her to visit her aunt in England. "About time you found out how the other half lives," he'd said in that deadpan way of his that Thorny could never quite decide was joking. And then, of course, Miriam had chimed in with the usual stuff about travel being broadening and how she had better get a new raincoat, and nobody had noticed that Thorny herself didn't have a thing to say.

Patrick saw her face and suddenly felt ashamed. After all, it wasn't her fault she was here.

He changed the subject before Thorny was forced to speak. "Did you hear the geese last night?"

"What geese?"

"Clarks', across the road." He grinned. "Mr. Clark must've forgot to latch their pen. They got out, the whole lot of them, honking like fun. Must've been after you shut your window, if you didn't hear. And goose mess all over the street—whew! Mr. Clark's been hunting them since five."

"I hope he found them all," Thorny said politely.

"So does Mum. She swears they kept her awake for hours last night. But you know Mum, she'll swear to—or at—almost anything." He grinned in such a friendly way that Thorny had to smile back. "Come on," he said then. "Even if you're not hungry, you'll have to eat something, just to satisfy Mum. And Millie Hill will be here soon, so you'd better hurry. She's from London, and curious as they come. She'd keep you here answering questions all day if she could."

"Miriam's like that," Thorny said half shyly. "My stepmother."

"Grim," Patrick said sympathetically. They left the room together. "Doesn't it bother your Dad?"

45

"She's not like that when Dad's around. She knows what he likes."

"Anything to please the boss," Patrick nodded.

There wasn't time for Thorny to reply. They were already in the kitchen. It was full of light and smelled like bacon and broiled tomatoes. To Thorny's surprise, she found she was hungry.

"Good morning, Thorny," Aunt Jenny smiled, turning from the stove with her curls in damp little wisps. "Two eggs or one?"

"Two, please," Thorny answered, avoiding Patrick's glance. "Can I help?"

"Another day," Jenny said. "Today you'd better just concentrate on eating. Mrs. Hill will be here in a few minutes, and I'm sure Patrick's told you about her." Her eyes were twinkling. "I suppose you aren't still hungry, are you, Patrick? I've made another couple of eggs."

"Pity to throw them out," he said, helping himself.

"So what are you and Thorny going to do this morning?" Jenny asked quite casually, but with a look in her eyes that Patrick didn't miss. His heart sank. He had plans for this morning. Right after breakfast he was meeting Alec at the Circle, and they were going to work on mapping the rest of the earth-forces. And then he was going to borrow the Robson's dog to see if it really did prefer to walk over the lines of earth-force, as Alec had said.

He gave his mother a speaking look. "*I'm* going out with Alec," he said.

"I thought I'd take a walk," Thorny put in quickly.

Jenny shook her head. "Sorry, you two, but it's no good. I know it's the fashion not to poke elbows into someone else's head-space—stop groaning, Patrick, if I'm behind on my slang it's because you are—but I'm afraid it's just not on. For the first few days at least I want you and Thorny to

46

stick together. You'd both rather do almost anything else, I imagine, but with all the lunatics on the loose and Belman on the warpath and Thorny not knowing her way around yet, it just doesn't make sense any other way.''

Thorny glared into her teacup, humiliated and relieved at the same time. After a moment Patrick shrugged. "I don't suppose Alec will mind you helping us," he told Thorny. "Do you like dogs?''

She looked up. "Is Alec a dog?"

Patrick laughed. But before he could explain, the kitchen door burst open. "Wotcher fink, Jen?" an excited voice said.

"Millie," Patrick mouthed to Thorny. The newcomer was a short, chirpy little woman who hardly paused for breath before launching into her news.

"'Ave you 'eard? Aht i' the garden I was, pickin' peas an' mindin' me manners, an' 'ere comes that Belman, perlite as yer please but no stoppin' 'im, callin' for that nob at the White 'Orse. You know the one—''

"The archaeologist?" Patrick got in, while Mrs. Hill took a slurp from the teacup Jenny handed her. "Atworthy?"

"No. T'uvver one. Bloke wiv the lines.''

"Oh, the ley-hunter. Kingsley.''

"That's 'im. Come outside, 'e did, still chewin' on 'is kipper. An' Belman, ever so quiet, goin' on and on about 'ow 'e'd made them threats, an' did 'e 'ave anyfink to do wiv it, an if so, 'ow. An' Kingsley, 'e's standin' there tryin' ter figger it all aht—''

"Figure what out, Mildred? For heaven's sake, what did Belman think he'd done?"

"Coo, Jen, wotcher fink? Bring back the Keystone, wot else?''

"You mean it's back?" Jenny pushed back her chair, but Thorny sat still, almost turned to stone herself.

"Wot 'ave I just bin tellin' you? Come back, it 'as, last night. Late, it was. Must've been after midnight. Askews walked their dog by the Circle just on the 'ahr, an' the Keystone was still away then. But it's back nah, straight up an' bold as the Queen o' Sheba in its old spot."

"Was it Kingsley who brought it back?" Jenny asked delightedly.

"'E says not, but 'oo knows? Wot wiv the Clarks' geese an' the dogs 'owlin' an' all, there's some that say it took more'n a crane ter get it there. Magic, my 'Arry finks. 'Alf give me a turn, 'im sayin' that."

"Gracious," Jenny said.

Patrick jumped to his feet. "I'm going to look." As an afterthought he turned to his cousin. "You coming, Thorny?"

Without a word she joined him. Her thoughts were buzzing. The Keystone had returned, just as the lady in white had said it would. The eclipse was one thing—the lady might have read about that—but this was something else again. How could she have known someone would bring the Keystone back? Unless, maybe, she had done it herself. . . . But could she? Hurrying down the road after Patrick, Thorny tried to imagine the white lady working that crane. It was impossible. Besides, how could she have gotten chains under that stone all on her own?

Thorny plucked at Patrick's arm and they stopped just by the main drive of the White Horse. "How much does the Keystone weigh?" she asked, frowning so worriedly it surprised him.

"A lot," he replied. He, too, had been thinking. "You'd need a crane. Belman has one, but I can't imagine him leaving it sitting around for somebody else to borrow. So someone must have got hold of another one afterwards." He grinned happily. "What a super idea, to pay Belman back in kind like that! I wish I'd thought of it."

"So you don't think it was—?"

"Magic?" He raised his brows. "Do you?"

"No. I just—"

"There's not a lot of that sort of thing around any more, is there?" He shrugged regretfully. "I wonder about Kingsley, though. Millie said he denied doing it. And he didn't look to me like a liar."

A tall, thin man came rushing out of the inn. Patrick saw him and waved. "That's Alec," he said. "I wonder if he knows about the Keystone? Come on. He's a bit gruff at first, but he's really quite decent. I'll vouch for you, so that's all right."

And Thorny, who had far more distressing things on her mind than being vouched for by Patrick, followed.

7

An Alliance

"I'm sorry, Patrick, but we're going to have to postpone our plans. Yes, I know the Keystone's come back. Stop sputtering."

Alec spoke quite calmly, but he was looking at Thorny. It was a thorough, intense look, neither friendly nor unfriendly. She returned it, trying to feel resentful. Patrick watched the two of them looking at each other. He felt like a spectator at a team sport. "Hey," he said after a minute, and then, when they both turned to him, didn't know what else to say. He gave a flustered cough.

"Friend of yours, Patrick?" Alec asked, giving Thorny a smile. She smiled back, but warily.

"She's my cousin," Patrick recovered. "But look, Alec, you don't really want to put off the rest of our mapping, do you? Belman knows about the Keystone being back. Once he gets his slaves back here he won't rest until it's gone again, and probably the whole Circle with it. This may be our last chance."

"Yesterday the mapping was important," Alec said, "because I wasn't sure about something. Now that the Keystone's come back everything's different." He turned to Thorny. "What did you say your name was?"

"Thorny."

His eyes narrowed. "Hawthorn, you mean. It is Hawthorn, isn't it?" She nodded, frowning. How did he know? Alec was quiet for a moment. "Why are you here?" he asked abruptly.

50

"Her Dad's on his honeymoon," Patrick answered for her, a bit too loudly. "She needed a place to stay."

Alec didn't seem to hear. "Hawthorn," he murmured. He shot a sharp look at Thorny. "Seen any strangers since you've been here? Anybody . . . really odd?" When she said nothing, he added, "A woman . . . white clothing, beautiful . . . or maybe she'd seem very old and ugly."

Thorny stared at him. How did he know about the white lady?

"Then you have seen her." Alec nodded, clearly very worried. "I thought so. She wants you to help, doesn't she?"

"Help how?" Patrick said loudly. "Who're you talking about?" Suddenly he guessed. "Hey, was that the woman who disappeared on you yesterday, Thorny?"

This got Alec's attention. "Did you see her, Patrick?"

"Well, not exactly. She'd gone by the time I—"

"Thorny," Alec said. "Promise me something."

"What?" she said nervously.

"Don't . . . let yourself get caught up. Don't do anything she says, anything at all. I haven't got time to explain right now. I have to do some checking . . . but I promise I'll tell you everything later. All right?"

"How do you know about her?" Thorny demanded.

"Later."

Her voice rose slightly. "Just tell me one thing. Everything she said is crazy, isn't it?"

Patrick frowned. What was going on here? Alec hesitated. Then he shook his head and took Thorny's arm, pulling her back into the shadow of the inn. Patrick followed. If they didn't want him, they'd have to tell him so.

Carefully Alec looked up and down the street. It was still quite early, and the street was deserted except for a woman going into Jefferson's grocery. Thorny was rigid, chewing her lip.

"I want you to see something," Alec said. Releasing her arm he pulled a circular object out from under the neck of his shirt. Then he lifted it over his head and pressed it into her hand.

"Come on, Alec," Patrick said impatiently. "Stop putting us on. It's just your compass."

"It is precisely because you think so," Alec said quietly, "that you will never be able to dowse. What do you see, Hawthorn?"

She was holding the object gingerly, staring into it. Patrick crowded over to look, too. It was fairly small, a little bigger than a man's watch. Now that he was examining it more closely, Patrick could see that it was thinner than an ordinary compass, about twice the thickness of a coin. A recessed dial and needle were protected by a glass top just like a regular compass, though the casing was made of a copper-coloured metal. At first glance the dial seemed perfectly normal, but the longer Patrick looked the less solid it seemed. There was something he wasn't seeing, but no matter how he tried, it wouldn't come clear.

"Well?" Alec said.

Thorny looked up. "What is it?" she whispered. "All those lights. And that shape . . ." The lights were pale and bright like little dots of moonlight patterning the dial of the compass. The pattern was unfamiliar: a circle bisected by the letter S, the dark half as beautiful and strange as the light. She bent her head, drawn to it even as she resisted it. She didn't see Patrick's frown, or Alec nodding with satisfaction.

"I thought so," he said. "Hang it around your neck, child."

'You're giving it to me?" Thorny asked, startled.

"It's a loan, not a gift. I may have to pay a visit today to somebody who wants it rather too much, and it'd be better off out of arm's reach. I'll get it back from you when I return. If I'm not back right away, you might need to—" He broke off, clearing his throat.

"Need to what?" Thorny asked, high and thin.

He shook his head. "Nothing. Just keep the medallion safe. Don't let anyone know you've got it." He gave her a commanding look. "Do you promise?"

Uncertainly, she nodded. First the white lady and now Alec. Who else was going to demand her to promise something without bothering to tell her why?

"Why does *she* get to—?" Patrick began, but Alec was already turning away.

"Sorry, Patrick," he said. "There's no time right now. But I need something from you. It's very important."

"What?" Patrick's resentment faded. Alec's voice was deadly serious.

"I want you to keep a good watch over Hawthorn."

Thorny frowned. "Hey, I don't need a babysitter."

Alec ignored her. "Keep her away from Belman, Patrick."

"Keep her—But why? What's going on?"

"Later," Alec said. He began to turn away, heading for the parking lot.

Patrick called after him. "Just keep her away from Belman?" he asked. "Not from that weird woman, too?"

Alec paused. "I don't think," he said quietly, "you'll be able to do anything about that one."

And then he was gone.

"So what was that all about?" Patrick asked after a moment.

Thorny shoved her hands in her pockets. "Don't ask me!" she snapped. "Nobody bothers to explain anything to me. Hawthorn do this and Hawthorn do that, and a bunch of it in my dresser drawer. Why don't you all just leave me alone?"

"I only asked what was going on," Patrick said huffily. "You're the one everyone's making a fuss of. If you don't know, who does?"

"Well, I don't. I don't know a thing."

"You talked to that weird woman, didn't you?"

"So what?"

"So didn't she say anything?"

"Oh, yeah, she said a lot of things. The trouble is, none of it makes any sense."

They were silent then, eyeing each other like two cats. "It might make sense to me," Patrick pointed out stubbornly. "You're not the only one with brains."

Thorny looked at her cousin. She sighed. "It started with that hawthorn bouquet. I found it in my room yesterday. The white lady said she put it there."

"She broke into our house?" Patrick said, aghast.

"To welcome me," Thorny said sourly.

"Just for that? To welcome you? She must be crazy!"

"That's what I keep telling myself," Thorny said shakily. "But Alec doesn't seem to think so, does he?"

"What else did the woman tell you?"

She leaned forward, sniffing a geranium beside the wall of the inn. For a long moment Patrick thought she wasn't going to answer. Then she looked up. "Do you think," she asked hesitantly, "there are some people who can know the future?"

"Fortune-tellers, you mean?"

"No, not fortune-tellers. The real thing. Really knowing that something . . . bad . . . is going to happen."

He frowned. "I don't know," he said slowly. "I've heard of people predicting airline crashes before they happen, or one of a pair of twins knowing the other's in danger, but . . . Did your white lady predict something awful?"

"It's all so crazy," Thorny muttered. "The trouble is, she knew a lot. About me, I mean. My real name, my age, the room I was going to sleep in, the fact that I was coming here at all. Even a lot of stuff about my parents. And I just don't know how she could."

"Mmm," Patrick said. "Most of the village did know you were coming. But she wasn't from the village, was she?"

Thorny described her, and Patrick shook his head. "Definitely not a villager. Which means she didn't hear about you from us."

"So how did she know all that?"

The question hung on the air. "She might have put a detective on you."

"But why?"

Patrick shrugged. "You said she was crazy, didn't you?"

"You should have heard her. It was like someone in the Bible, all thee's and thou's. That was bad enough. But then she said she had an ancient enemy who was trying to destroy her, and that he was going to end up destroying the earth instead. And—this is the worst part—Patrick, she called herself a goddess!"

Patrick's brows went up. "Good grief."

"I know. I thought exactly the same thing. Except that there was something about her—" She broke off, chewing her lip. "Anyway, then she said it all hinged on Awen-Un, that it was the . . . I don't know, the centre of control, I think she said. She said something about being able to protect it for a while, but once the moon gets eaten by darkness, that'll be it. The green will all die, and there'll be fires and floods—" It was all pouring out now, faster and faster. "And I know what she means by 'eaten by darkness.' It's just got to be the eclipse on Friday night! And today's Wednesday. But the thing that bothers me the most, Patrick—"

"You mean there's more?"

"—the thing I just can't understand, is how she could've known the Keystone would come back after Belman took it away."

Patrick took a deep breath. "She knew that?"

"She said it would happen. Not just once, but twice! It's after the second time that everything's supposed to fall apart."

Patrick wiped sweat off his forehead. "The test will be what happens after Belman gets the Keystone out again. If he does."

"You mean, if it comes back a second time, like she said . . . Patrick, you don't think she could have moved it back herself, do you?"

"Somebody must have," he said. "And if it was anybody ordinary, we're bound to find out. You can't keep a big job like that a secret in a village. You'd need a crane and half a dozen strong men at least to help. Someone's bound to talk. And if they don't, then . . . well, we'll know the . . . the other thing."

"That whoever moved it isn't ordinary, you mean," she said leadenly.

"And that your lady isn't mad, either." The thought stuck like a lump in his throat. He swallowed. If the white lady wasn't mad, if everything she said was true . . .

Suddenly the hairs on his neck prickled. Someone was watching them. He turned his head, hackles rising. It was Belman astride that black mare of his. He must have ridden here, but Patrick hadn't heard a thing. Neither, from the look of her, had Thorny. She was as startled as a rabbit frozen in headlights. Belman smiled at Thorny, not seeming to see Patrick standing protectively in front of her. "So I'm finally seeing my new neighbour," he said, warm and dark as fruitcake. "How long have you been in Wychwood Mount?"

Thorny flushed. "I just got here yester—"

Patrick pushed his way in. "I didn't think you were all that interested in your neighbours, Mr. Belman."

Briefly Belman let his eyes rest on Patrick. "Patrick Newport," he said thoughtfully. "You would be surprised at the things that interest me." He urged his mare closer to them, looking at Thorny again. Patrick shot a quick glance her way and was shocked at how uncertain she looked. *Keep her away from Belman*, Patrick thought, and burst in desperately again.

"Thorny and I have to go now. We—"

"Thorny?" Belman queried. His strange mouth quirked at Thorny. "That's not really your name, is it?"

"It's short for Hawthorn," she said defiantly, and then added, "It's a bad luck name."

"Names aren't bad luck," Belman said. "Only namegivers, sometimes." He gave her a smile so kind, so understanding, she found it hard to look away.

Patrick blinked. What was going on? The two of them were talking as if they'd known each other for years. He scowled at her, trying to make her meet his eyes, but it was no good. "Don't forget Mum's expecting us, Thorny," he lied loudly.

"Mothers can be difficult," Belman said, still to Thorny. "They want their own lives, whatever *we* want, but in the end they still try to pull the reins on ours."

Involuntarily Thorny's hands clenched. *They want their own lives.* Four years ago Dad had said that with the same tone, the same bitterness; though his face had not been nearly so gentle. She put her hands behind her to hide their trembling, and looked at the ground. It was hard to believe this was the same ruthless man who wanted to destroy Awen-Un.

The black mare made a sudden skittish move sideways, and Belman tightened the reins. "Do you like horses?" he asked, seeing Thorny watching.

"I don't know anything about them. This one seems . . . nervous."

"She likes to please me," Belman shrugged. "But basically it isn't her nature to be docile. Would you care to ride her?"

"Well, I'm not very—"

"I'll put you up in front of me. Your little weight won't make much difference to the horse. You could come with me to Awen-Un and have a look at this magical stone of mine."

Thorny hesitated. Patrick wanted to shake her. She was actually thinking about going with him! He reached for Thorny's arm and began marching her towards the road. "I told you, Mum's expecting us," he said loudly, his fingers tightening as he felt Thorny hang back. What was wrong with her, for heaven's sake?

Thorny looked back at Belman looming above her, all planes and angles and warm, gentle eyes. She didn't really want to go with him, but for a moment she was almost tempted. It would serve Patrick right, she told herself, pushing her around like this.

And then, suddenly, a cloud went over the sun, and Belman changed. She saw his eyes, unclouded now by the glitter of reflected sunlight, and it was like looking into dead ash after a fire. Shocked, she let Patrick pretend to turn her in the direction of home. Behind them she heard the clop-clop-clop of Belman's horse cantering away. She felt as if she had just escaped a serious accident.

8

Of Sun and Moon
and Standing Stones

It was still fairly early, not quite ten o'clock, but the village was no longer quiet. Word of the Keystone's return was spreading like wildfire. Towards the crossroads, more and more villagers were coming out of their homes and gathering in the street, chattering like children. There weren't many strangers about yet. Almost all of yesterday's protestors had driven in only for the day, and most of the London newspapermen who had stayed at the inn had gone home after the rally, thinking the excitement was all over. But at least two of the inn's guests were still here, Patrick saw: the ley-hunter called Kingsley, standing on the steps of the White Horse, and with him the bad-tempered Professor Atworthy. June Avery, who helped her husband Tom run the inn, was listening openly, standing at the door with her shopping basket over her arm.

"Come on," Patrick whispered to Thorny, jerking his head towards the two men. "I want to hear."

"I thought we were going to see the Keystone?"

"Yes, but not now. Belman's going there, and in case you've forgotten, you're supposed to stay away from him." He eyed her challengingly, but she said nothing. After a moment he shrugged and headed for Kingsley and Atworthy. Thorny followed reluctantly. Something else she had to do because somebody told her, she thought resentfully.

"—absolute belly gargle!" Atworthy was saying as they came up. "A four-ton stone simply does not hoist itself up and walk away all on its own! As a fellow academic you should be helping me scotch these ridiculous stories, not encourage them!"

"I've never said the Keystone came back on its own," Kingsley protested. "All I've said is that it wouldn't be the first time people thought a stone moved by itself."

"Balderdash!"

"Folklore *is* my specialty, Atworthy. I can cite you dozens of cases. At le Menec, in France, there are half a dozen stones that are supposed to walk down regularly to the local stream to drink, killing anyone who gets in their way. And there's a stone at Banbury which is said to hear the church clock strike twelve, at which time it goes off to—"

"Spare me the details. The point is not what the great unwashed *think* happens—"

"But why do they think so? There must be some reason why legends like that persist. It isn't just stones moving, either, it's stones refusing to be moved. Becoming impossibly heavy, say, or turning over and killing the person trying to move them, or bringing bad luck—"

"Or arranging for someone like you to bring them back when they *are* moved?" Atworthy said nastily. "It wasn't very wise of you to threaten Belman like that yesterday, if that's what you had in mind."

Jeremy Kingsley shrugged. "Except that it wasn't, I'm sorry to say. As I pointed out to Belman, I was at the rally until after shop closing time, so even if I had thought of it, I couldn't have arranged to rent a crane in time to use it last night."

"Unless," Atworthy said, "you'd arranged for a crane beforehand."

60

"On the offchance that Belman would get his permission and cart off the Keystone all in one day?" Kingsley laughed. "I'm scarcely organized enough to grade my term papers on time! No, I'm sorry, but if you're looking for someone with that kind of foresight, it's not me."

"It's not anybody, and that's flat," June Avery put in unexpectedly. "Hasn't been a crane rental except Belman's in the whole of the shire. That reporter in our Number Three's been checking, and Aggie Millson says—"

"Mrs. Millson runs the telephone exchange," Patrick whispered to Thorny. "She listens in."

"My dear woman," Atworthy said. "My dear, dear woman. Whatever your Aggie Millson says, that stone did not return on its own. Rest assured, a crane was used. Maybe rented from someone out of the shire, maybe stolen from Belman—"

"His was locked up," Kingsley said calmly. "He told me so himself."

"And besides," June began, "there couldn't have been—"

"Clearly," Professor Atworthy said wearily, "I am wasting my time. You will believe what you want, no matter how senseless it is."

Patrick couldn't contain himself any longer. "Did anyone see a crane go by in the middle of the night?" He hadn't lived in a village all his life without knowing that the unusual rarely passed unnoticed.

"That's just what I was trying to say," June said, her colour high. "Wasn't even a tractor moving here last night. Jeffersons were up all night with young Susan's mumps, and they'd have seen anything on the A-road. And Amelia Green was watching this one. Her insomnia—"

"Insomniacs and lunatics!" Atworthy said. "You're well left to one another." He gave an exaggerated bow. "My bill, please."

"You're checking out?" June said woodenly.

"It is," Atworthy pronounced, "the usual reason for asking for one's bill." And they disappeared inside.

"Whew!" Patrick said. "What a puffed-up old phony!"

"He is difficult," Jeremy Kingsley nodded. "He's like so many scientists, wanting cast-iron proof for everything. To him standing stones are tools or monuments, nothing more."

"What else could they be?" Thorny asked hesitantly, thinking of the white lady's prophecy. "I mean, could a stone circle mean something else besides just . . . well, a bunch of stones standing together?"

Kingsley fished a pipe out of his pocket. "Now that depends on whom you ask," he grinned. "If you ask me, you ought to keep in mind that to most archaeologists I'm a traitor even to mention the old folk theories."

"But you're just as much a professor as they are, aren't you?" Patrick asked.

"Oh, yes, I am a professor. Not of archaeology, though, as Atworthy would hasten to say! I specialize in British folklore. It's a branch of study where stone circles take quite a prominent part." A battered car full of strangers came careening down the street, camera gear poking out the window. "Press," Kingsley grimaced. "Didn't take very long for them to get wind of the Keystone's return, did it?" The car pulled up beside the inn, but before anyone could get out, Kingsley took Thorny and Patrick by the arm and hustled them inside. "We'll go into the private lounge," he said. "They can't bother us in there."

Even before they were settled, Patrick was asking questions. "Did you really mean it when you said standing stones don't like to be moved, Professor Kingsley? Or were you just getting at Atworthy?"

"Call me Jeremy. And you are—?" Patrick introduced himself and Thorny. Jeremy smiled. "Well, then, Patrick, I do like to get at Professor Atworthy. I guess it's pretty obvious! But just the same, the things I said about the standing stones were quite true. Through all the ages of folk history we see the same theme over and over again: move the stones at your peril!'' He stretched out comfortably in an armchair.

"But why?'' Thorny asked, her voice tense. "What's so dangerous about moving a few old stones?''

"Why were they put there in the first place, Thorny?'' Jeremy replied. "That's really the answer to your question.''

"You mean, because the stones were meant to do some kind of job in that particular spot?''

"Something like that,'' Jeremy nodded.

"Then the earth a stone stands on is more important than the stone itself?''

Jeremy took his time about answering. "I wouldn't exactly say that,'' he replied at last. "The earth under the standing stones is important, all right. But so are the stones themselves. Most of these stones have electromagnetic properties, you know. To put it simply, that means electricity can flow through them. If there are electromagnetic currents in the earth, and some people believe there are, then the stones might have been placed where they are in order to pick up on those currents. Sort of like—''

"I know,'' Patrick interrupted. "Like antennas picking up radio signals.''

Jeremy looked surprised. "Exactly. Sharp of you, Patrick.''

"I know somebody who's a dowser,'' Patrick said nonchalantly. "He talked about it a bit while I was helping him yesterday.''

"Are you saying,'' Thorny asked, trying to understand, "that early men knew about these electric currents in the earth and put the stones at the most powerful places on purpose?''

"It's one theory,'' Jeremy said cautiously.

"But what *for*?''

Jeremy shrugged. "That's the hard question. One hears so much rubbish about that, it's hard to separate the gold from the dross. Things like prehistoric priests draining off the power of the stones for their own purposes. That's a variation on the old utopia idea, of course. The Golden Age, with men at harmony with nature and with each other, and the priests busy using the earth-forces to keep everything nice; even moving the actual currents somewhere else, if they didn't happen to like them where they were. Or there's another crazy idea that the earth-forces and the stones made up some kind of prehistoric communications network for UFO's."

"Alec—he's the dowser I told you about—he said they used the stones like lightning rods," Patrick said, "putting them over the most dangerous places to conduct any overload of electricity out into the air where it can't do much harm."

"I've heard that theory, too," Jeremy nodded. "Supposedly the major currents of earth-force are like rivers of water. With lots of other currents running into them, they get bigger and bigger. Eventually the power gets so strong and so dangerous, it has to be controlled. Hence the stones."

"So places like Awen-Un, with lots of stones—?"

"Would be major control centres," Jeremy nodded. "So the theory goes, anyway."

Awen-Un, the first, the mother of all circles, the centre of control. Thorny shook her head. No. "All this stuff about control centres, it is just a theory, isn't it, Jeremy? I mean, there must be other reasons for circles like Awen-Un."

Jeremy nodded. "Atworthy would say they were used as prehistoric churches. I think that's much too simplistic, myself, but there's probably some truth in it. The earliest primitive religion we know anything about was the worship of a moon goddess—" Thorny gave an involuntary jerk, but Jeremy was lighting his pipe and didn't notice— "who was also the goddess of the earth. Stones were sacred because they were thought to be the Earth Goddess's bones, and a circle was sacred because it was the Moon Goddess's shape at full moon. So you can see why a stone circle would have been a perfect place for the worship of an Earth-Moon goddess." He puffed absently on his pipe. "Stones have been credited with incredible powers throughout history, you know. Things like healing and fertility, mainly, which have always been the White Goddess's things."

"White Goddess?" Patrick frowned.

"We sometimes call her that. In folklore she often appears to people with white skin and white hair. Very beautiful, though, especially her blue eyes." Thorny and Patrick studiously avoided looking at each other. "That's her mother-form," Jeremy went on. "But sometimes she shows up as an owl, or a deer, or even a white horse. Sometimes she's a young girl, and other times she's an old hag. In her human form she was actually a kind of a prehistoric trinity. We sometimes call her the goddess of three and nine."

Thorny went white. *I am three and I am nine.* She made a sudden and abrupt movement towards the window, as if to get some air.

"Are you all right?" Jeremy asked in concern.

"It's just that it's so hot." She took a deep breath of stale air. "Three what, and nine what?" she asked then. "This goddess, I mean."

Jeremy's brows quirked at her, but he answered readily enough. "As Goddess of Three, she was Earth, Moon and Underworld. The Nine come in as subgroups of these. To give you an example, as Earth she was the seasons—spring, or the young girl I told you about; harvest, or the mother, bearing fruit; and winter, or the hag. She's a crescent moon when she is the young girl, the full moon when she's the mother, and she wanes to new moon when she's the hag. That's when she stands for death."

Thorny was looking very white again. Patrick knew what she was thinking. He was rather bothered by it himself.

"Do you believe all this, Jeremy?" he challenged. "Did people in the Stone Age really use Awen-Un to worship some scary white lady who runs the moon and the earth?"

"I don't know," Jeremy said carefully. "It's a reasonable idea, more reasonable than most. But I'd be less than honest if I didn't say that I rather like the earth-current/lightning-rod theory, too. I touched a standing stone once on Bodmin Moor in Cornwall and got the worst electric shock of my life." He shrugged. "Let's just say I'm keeping an open mind. One thing I am sure of is that at least a few of the stones in most circles were placed where they were for astronomical reasons. If you stood back in a place where they lined up and looked to where they pointed on the horizon, you'd see something special at just the right time of the year. Sunrise at midsummer, for instance, or the most northerly winter moonrise."

"I heard you arguing with Atworthy about that," Patrick nodded.

"Believe it or not, we agree more on that than on anything else," Jeremy grinned. "The trouble is, he only believes in sun alignments, not moon alignments, like I do. He thinks the builders of the circles would have been more interested in the sun than the moon, because of them worshipping a sun god. If he knew folklore, he'd realize the sun god was an upstart, coming along ages and ages after the moon goddess. Of course, the sun god eventually became just as important to prehistoric peoples as the moon goddess, but that wasn't until long after the earliest circles were built." He rubbed his forehead absently. "It's the earliest ones that I think have moon alignments. Take Awen-Un, for instance. If I could get a proper survey made of its stones, I'm pretty sure it would show moon lines."

Thorny was staring miserably out the window. She had stopped listening. All she had wanted was to write off the white lady and her words as a lunatic delusion. She might have succeeded, too, in spite of the eclipse, in spite of the Keystone coming back. But not now. Jeremy Kingsley had made that impossible. *I am three and I am nine*, the lady had said, and there was Jeremy's prehistoric trinity, the Goddess of Three and Nine. His description of her was a dead match for the woman Thorny had seen. Stones moving by themselves—and why not, if they were her bones, and the goddess wished it? The white lady insisting her goddess-like powers would protect the earth except when the moon was eclipsed—and Jeremy saying his goddess had power over both earth and moon. The way she had said Awen-Un was the centre of control.

No, it could not all be coincidence.

9

Flowers for Thorny

"It really can't be anything else, can it? Your white lady, Jeremy's goddess . . ."

Once again they were out on the street. The car full of reporters had been joined by several others, their occupants clamoring for rooms, information and beer. As Patrick and Thorny left, June was too busy at the registration desk even to wave.

It had been hot in the lounge, but out on the street the sun simply beat down, a ball of blinding white dominating the cloudless sky. No one else was outside. Even the gossipers had taken shelter indoors. The flowers in the inn's front garden were curling like burning paper, dying in their beds. The lawn was yellow and sere, puddles of water lying uselessly on the surface from the hosing it had received that morning. *The green world withers and burns*, Thorny thought numbly. *A moon shining alone in an empty sky*. Was it really going to happen?

"She isn't a goddess. Patrick, she can't be!"

"You give me another explanation," he said.

Thorny thought desperately. "She probably read about Jeremy's white goddess, and since she happens to look a bit like her—"

"A bit!"

"—okay, then, a lot. So she decided to act the part. Or maybe she really thinks she is her. There're lots of people in mental hospitals who think they're somebody else. Or maybe she dyed her hair and used a lot of makeup, and this is all just a joke.''

"Did it feel like a joke?'' She was silent. "Anyway, what would be the point? What kind of charge would she get out of tricking a kid? And how did she know so much about you? And how about Alec warning you about her? *He* took her seriously enough, all right!''

"You don't know anything about Alec. He might be part of the whole plot. He might—''

Patrick gave a disgusted snort. "Come on, Thorny, Alec's not like that.''

She jammed her hands in her pockets, looking down. Under her shirt she felt the cool touch of Alec's medallion. Patrick was right. Alec wasn't like that. Whatever the white lady was or wasn't, Alec was on their side.

She looked at Patrick, her face miserable. "All right, then, she's a mental case. Either she is, or I am. I'm the only one who saw her, remember. Maybe I imagined the whole thing.''

"Pretty imaginative, thinking up a white lady who just happened to be exactly like Jeremy's goddess, and telling you Awen-Un was her circle, and that she was in charge of the moon and the earth, all *before* Jeremy told us anything about her!''

"Maybe I read about her somewhere.''

"Pigs might fly,'' Patrick said rudely. "And what about her knowing that the Keystone was going to come back?''

"If I imagined everything else, maybe I imagined she said that, too.''

"Give me a break!''

A long moment passed. Then Patrick said more calmly, "The point is, the Keystone did come back. And nobody stole Belman's crane, and there wasn't one brought in by road from anywhere else. So how did the stone get back? The only thing we know is that Jeremy says stones have sometimes moved by themselves. And if there's that much magic going on—and it's starting to look as if there is—why worry about a goddess or two?''

"If you were the one all this was happening to," Thorny said bitterly, "you wouldn't be so quick to jump at the idea of magic."

"I'm only being logical," Patrick protested. "Eliminate everything else, and whatever's left, no matter how unbelievable, must be the truth. Sherlock Holmes said that."

"So now you're Sherlock Holmes! Why don't you grow up? Don't you realize, if all of this *is* true, the world is going to die in two days, and there's nothing we can do to stop it? I told you what she said. If I don't save Awen-Un before the eclipse—"

"That's what she wanted you to do? Save Awen-Un?"

"Yes! And your precious Alec told me *not* to do what she says! Not that it makes much difference. I don't know how I could save it anyway, to say nothing of stopping her stupid enemy—"

Patrick grabbed her by the shoulders, so hard that she broke off in mid-rage, staring at him. "You never told me any of this."

"I did so! Her enemy's the one who's going to destroy the earth, while she's busy trying to save herself during the eclipse. I told you!"

"But you didn't tell me it was by stopping her enemy that you were supposed to save Awen-Un." He could hardly keep from shouting it aloud. "Thorny, don't you see what this means? It means Belman, that's what! Belman's the one trying to destroy Awen-Un, so Belman must be the enemy she was talking about. I always thought he was weird! No wonder Alec told us to keep you away from him!"

"You're crazy, Patrick! Belman may be trying to destroy Awen-Un, but he has his own reasons for that. It's got nothing to do with trying to hurt the white lady! Anyway, you're still assuming that she was telling me the truth—"

He threw his hands up in the air. "Why are you being so dumb? It's not as if Belman's even decent—"

"What's that got to do with it? He's just not the enemy the lady was talking about. For heaven's sake, Patrick, he's not even old!"

"That's what all the girls say."

"So what does that mean?"

"Nothing," Patrick muttered. "Forget it."

Thorny stared at him uncertainly. She could see that there were things about Belman some people might find attractive: his strength, his understanding, his interest in people. Even Aunt Jenny said that Belman could be charming. But that didn't mean she liked him! "I don't like Belman," she told Patrick defiantly. "And anyway, it's none of your business."

"It's my business if you make a fool of yourself over him instead of stopping him from destroying Awen-Un like the lady wants!"

She whitened. "So now I'm a fool. Thanks a lot. You'd better save Awen-Un, since I'm so dumb."

Patrick stuck his hands in his pockets. "Sorry," he muttered. "It's just that when he talked to you, you seemed . . . oh, I don't know, kind of . . . well, kind of like a rabbit being looked at by a snake, you know?"

A rabbit being looked at by a snake. Some apology that was! Thorny tugged at her hair.

"I'm not going to talk about Belman any more," she announced. "I'm going back to Aunt Jenny's, and I'm going to have lunch, and I'm not going to talk. So there!" And with that she began to march away.

Slowly Patrick followed her home. Cucumber sandwiches and civilization; and the eclipse just two days away. Why did it have to be Thorny that things were happening to, when he could have handled it so much better?

Shortly before one, Patrick saw Belman through the kitchen window, cantering up the lane to the side door of Stratton Hall. Because of the hedge, Patrick lost sight of him as he dismounted, but in a little while Belman's mare came into view, led towards the stables by the man called Red. Belman had one other servant, a greasy-looking fellow who made a point of staying indoors. No one else in the village seemed to know he existed, but Patrick had seen him: once shaking a dust cloth out of the Hall's side door, and once throwing potato peelings out the back kitchen door. This last Patrick had seen from the secret tunnel he and Mike Stratton had made long ago in the hedge behind the zodiac, and which Patrick still used when he wanted to be alone. He had wondered then why a man like Belman, who obviously had plenty of money, put up with so second-class a servant as this Greaser.

Patrick turned away from the window, looking impatiently at Thorny. She was still sitting over her tea, listening to Jenny reading bits of the newspaper out loud.

"And here's another one," Jenny was saying. "Plane sucked into whirlwind over Bermuda Triangle. Two hundred people missing, presumed dead. Can you believe the number of disasters, all in one night? Two major plane crashes, a mud-slide, an earthquake—"

"You finished, Thorny?" Patrick interrupted. He jerked his head significantly towards the Hall. "We did want to see the Keystone, didn't we?"

The gesture was not lost on Jenny. "Keeping out of Belman's way, are you?" she asked shrewdly. The two cousins were silent. Jenny frowned. "You aren't planning on doing anything silly, I hope? If you think Belman won't find out—"

They hadn't said a word to her about the white lady. Thorny had thought about telling her, but she was Patrick's mother, and Patrick had shown no indication of wanting her advice. In a way Thorny envied him. He was so sure of himself, making up his own mind about things without caring too much what other people thought, or bothering with niceties like being polite and getting permission.

"Don't worry about Belman, Mum," Patrick said smoothly. "We're not exactly stupid, you know."

"Are you sure?" Jenny asked. "It'd be an awful nuisance to have to get someone to defend the pair of you in a court of law."

"My dear mother," Patrick said. "My dear, dear mother—"

Jenny laughed. She went to answer a knock at the door, returning with an enormous bundle wrapped in florist paper. "Mmm," she sniffed. "What a gorgeous smell!"

"Pong, you mean," Patrick said, ostentatiously holding his nose.

His mother held the parcel out to Thorny. "Flowers for you, Thorny. Lucky girl!"

For a moment Thorny didn't move, remembering the bouquet of hawthorn. If this was another one of those . . .

Clearly Patrick remembered it, too. "Who's it from?" he demanded, not joking now. "Go on, Thorny, read the card."

She let her eyes drop to the little envelope attached to the parcel. It had the address of a Swindon flower shop on it, and her name typed on the front. That looked all right, but you never knew. Carefully, keeping her face hidden, she withdrew the card from inside.

"Thorny, dear," it said. "They're not violets, but I didn't have much choice—Swindon isn't New York! Missing you, and much love, Dad."

"They're from Dad!" she exclaimed, looking up happily. She tore open the paper, revealing an extravagant arrangement of orchids and yellow roses. Their exotic scent permeated the room, far removed from the comfortable sausage-smell of lunch.

"From your father?" Patrick asked. "But why?"

Thorny was bending over the bouquet. "The card said he was missing me," she said, her voice muffled.

"On his honeymoon, and missing his kid?"

"But aren't they lovely?" Jenny hurried in. "Do you know, I think the last time I got hothouse flowers they were from John? It was years ago. We shared lodgings in London, you know, after our parents here died. But I thought it was about time I got my own flat, and managed to get up the nerve to tell John. He didn't argue. He never did, but somehow I felt simply dreadful, anyway. And then I got this wonderful bunch of roses, all colours and smells . . ." She made a rueful face. "I've never felt so guilty in my life!"

"Was that why he sent them?" Patrick asked curiously. "So you would feel guilty?"

Thorny frowned angrily. Over her head Jenny made an annoyed face at Patrick. "Who knows what he meant?" she replied lightly. "Anyway, I ended up staying on with him. Until he met your mother, actually, Thorny. But then I'd decided it wasn't a flat I wanted, after all, but to come back here and marry Rob —"

"I thought you'd wanted that all along, but Uncle John said you were too young," Patrick said.

"No doubt I was," Jenny said firmly. "But by that time I was older, and—"

The telephone rang. "Not again!" Jenny complained. "That phone's been simply ringing off the wall today. What with the Clarks' geese and dogs barking all night and the Keystone's mysterious goings on . . ." She bustled away.

Thorny pushed her chair back and began to leave the room. "What're you up to?" Patrick asked.

"I'm going to write to my father," she said, her voice hard. "I want to thank him for my flowers."

"I thought we were going over to the Circle."

"I want to write Dad."

"Well, I'm not sitting around while you write letters that won't get out until tomorrow's post anyway. I'm going to go look at the Keystone while I still have a chance."

She glared at him, but Aunt Jenny came in before she could think of something really nasty to say. "You two clearing out?" she asked. "I've just been commandeered into baking for the hospital auxiliary meeting tomorrow. Mary can't do it, her little girl's had some kind of fainting fit, and Amelia Green's frantic with insomnia and a headache. There just isn't anyone else."

"Do you need some help?" Thorny offered.

"No, dear, thanks, but you go with Patrick."

"Thorny's not coming with me. She's going to write to her dad," Patrick said, his jaw jutting.

"Really?" Jenny said, looking at Thorny thoughtfully.

"I told her the post doesn't get out till tomorrow," Patrick said, "but she—"

"Thorny must do as she thinks best, Patrick," Jenny said. "Not everyone enjoys being ridden roughshod over, you know." She gave Thorny a little smile. "Sometimes you have to fight these men," she said, "if you want to call your soul your own."

Thorny looked again at the flowers. Roses, pale and prickly, bound with wire to those exotic orchids. The kind of thing you sent to a lover, she thought, not a daughter. Well, he had said he'd tried for violets. What was wrong with her, anyway? Dad had done something really nice, letting her know that she wasn't forgotten, reminding her that she was still his. Why, suddenly, did the whole thing seem wrong?

"Come on, Patrick," she said, turning abruptly away. "Let's go see that Keystone."

"What about your letter?"

She looked at the floor. "I've changed my mind."

And, for once, Patrick knew enough not to push it.

10

The Wishing Well

At the Circle, the same men who had dug the Keystone out of its socket and chained it to the crane the previous day were hard at it again. They looked in an ugly mood, Patrick thought, stripped to the waist and pouring with sweat, cursing loud enough to be heard even on the footpath. Today there were only a few onlookers. The general public didn't yet know about the Keystone's return, and the heat was keeping away most of the villagers. But Patrick saw Amelia Green, looking like a big grey mushroom under her sun-umbrella, snorting and puffing with outrage at the men's language. Mrs. Robson was there, too, with young Jim. Both of them were red-faced and miserable with heat, and Jim didn't even return Patrick's wave. Mike Jefferson was leaning on his bike, watching, while the vegetables he was supposed to be delivering wilted in the carrier. Most of the other people there were reporters. They were going to have a field day with this story, Patrick thought, watching one of them being strongarmed back onto public land by Belman's man, Red.

"We're not going to be able to get near the Keystone," Thorny said.

"Funny how it looks just the same," Patrick murmured. Greyish, lumpish, shiny where the lichen had been rubbed off, black where greasy hands had touched it, still it was the same stone he'd known all his life, sitting in its socket as if it had never been gone. There wasn't a thing about it that looked magical. Could it really have made its own way back across that huge stretch of open moor?

In the Circle one of the labourers tripped on a chain and fell, cursing vigorously. It was the final straw for Miss Green.

"Outrageous, simply outrageous," she declared, bearing down on Patrick and Thorny like an ocean liner on a pair of rowboats. "And children present!"

"Hullo, Miss Green," Patrick said, getting out of her way a little too late.

"You ought not to be here," she told him sternly. "Bad enough seeing such language printed word for word in tomorrow's papers, without having to listen to it, too. I shall ring for a constable if it doesn't stop at once."

A reporter came up, sniffing an interview. "What's the trouble?" he asked, licking his finger and turning a page in his notebook. "Peaceful British countryside invaded by four-letter words? Police suspect foul say?"

Miss Green looked at the young man with distaste. "You are, sir, a journalist?"

"Daily Howl."

"Then I have nothing to tell you."

"You and everybody else," the man said, shutting his notebook with a disgusted snort. "What I'm doing here half-way to bleeding Iceland watching a bloody great lump of rock just sit there—"

"Your language, sir!" Miss Green thundered. The reporter winced and backed off. Over in the Circle one of the Swindon labourers said something about foghorns. The others laughed rudely. "And we'll just see," Miss Green said magnificently, "how funny they find it when the police arrive." And she sailed indignantly off.

Mike pushed his bike over to join them. He was a skinny kid of about ten. His father was the village green-grocer. "Right old tartar," he said, nodding after Miss Green.

"How's your sister, Mike?" Patrick asked, remembering that June Avery had said young Susan was sick.

"Not so bad. Just mumps, innit? Kept us up, though. This your cousin from America?"

"Canada," Thorny said.

"Thorny, meet Mike. Mike, Thorny."

They nodded at one another. Thorny was thinking hard. "Were your parents really watching the street all night?" she asked. "They couldn't have missed seeing a crane bring the Keystone back?"

"Not likely," Mike shrugged. "Weren't no crane, anyway. None rented 'cept Belman's, and his locked up tight. . . . That stone came back by magic, 'less it's grown legs." He laughed.

There was another loud burst of swearing over at the Circle. "They sure aren't in a very good mood," Patrick said.

"Having to work a bit harder today 'n yesterday," Mike grinned. "At it since nine, they say. Got the Keystone out th'once, 'nen the chain broke an' it dropped right back into its hole. 'Nen they had to go all the way to Swindon for a new one, because Robson's wouldn't sell to them. Now this new one keeps slipping. Kind of put them in a temper, you might say."

The Keystone almost seemed to have a mind of its own, sliding sideways when the men wanted it upright, refusing to tilt when they heaved on it, settling down again just as they thought they had it secure.

Thorny and Patrick watched for quite some time, but still the battle between the men and the stone remained deadlocked. "All day job, this is," Mike shrugged at last. "An' I'm still in dirt with my da' over yesterday's deliveries." He threw a leg over his bicycle. "See you," he said, and pedaled off.

Thorny was finding it harder and harder to stay still. It was awful having to watch this—to witness, for the second time in two days, something terribly close to a murder. She wished she could pretend the Keystone was just an ordinary stone. But she couldn't. In a way that she couldn't explain, it seemed to reach out and demand something from her. Her hand crept upward, and under her shirt she felt the round shape of Alec's medallion. And then she turned her head and saw Belman.

Patrick saw him at the same moment. He was riding the black mare rather quickly and purposefully, not just sitting up on the rise like a baron surveying his domain.

"Let's get out of here," Patrick said.

She didn't protest, though for a moment he thought she might. "Where to?"

"Lady Copse," he said, and jerked his head towards it. It wasn't very far, a short distance away to the south and west. Nor was it very large. But it was old. Some said it was as old as any forest left in Britain. It had a wishing well, much sought out by tourists, though most of them came away disappointed by its simplicity, if they were not first turned back by the wood's wildness. Even the villagers rather avoided Lady Copse. But today it looked green and cool.

Thorny and Patrick wouldn't let themselves run from Belman, but they wasted no time getting away, either. Patrick didn't want to keep looking over his shoulder, but when they got to the northern edge of the wood, he allowed himself a quick glance. Belman had stopped beside the crane, but he wasn't watching his men, he was watching them.

"The path to the wishing well is farther down," Patrick told Thorny loudly, though he couldn't imagine Belman being able to hear. Still, for some reason it seemed important that Belman believe they were just being ordinary tourists, going into this wood.

It was amazingly cool under the shadow of the trees. The tourists kept the path fairly clear, but it was narrow, and it wound amid ferns, young willows and the stunted furze growing at the base of taller trees.

Thorny went after Patrick. She had never been in a wood like this. It wasn't like the few Canadian forests she had seen: the Pinery with its gritty openness and never-ending pines, seen on a school field trip; or the muskeg smell and clear rivers of Algonquin. Beside those Lady Copse was ancient; a mother of a forest aging into darkness and decay. She shivered. Neither she nor Patrick spoke. Thorny looked back, but all she could see were the gnarled, twisted trunks of trees receding into shadow, and hovering thickets of thorn.

The well wasn't anything like Thorny had expected. There was no raised brickwork, no hanging bucket, no picturesque little roof. It was merely an earth-hugging rock slab shaped like a picture frame around a rectangular opening full of water.

"You're supposed to pick a willow leaf the exact length of your palm," Patrick said, "then cup it in your hands, collect a little of the well water on it, and wish."

Thorny shook her head. "I don't want to."

He tried to grin. "Well, I'm going to. Maybe I'll ask to see your white lady, what do you think? Not that it'll work. It never does. I'll get a leaf for you, too, in case you change your mind." He hesitated, but she said nothing. A little helplessly he turned to look for a willow tree. There were none near the well. The only trees there were birch, tall, white and feminine. He disappeared into the trees, leaving Thorny by herself.

She watched him go, feeling very alone. Only when even the sound of him was gone did she approach the well. Uncertainly she knelt down, staring into its depths. For a moment she could see her own face, wide brown eyes, mouth soft and vulnerable, cheekbones high and shadowed like her father's.

And then, as if the sun had gone out and the moon had taken its place, her face dissolved. She watched, fascinated, seeing an image form and grow, recognizing only slowly what it was. A tree branch, but not birch; not with those shiny leaves and white flowers, that single sharp thorn. No, it was hawthorn. But there was no hawthorn growing nearby to let itself be reflected.

The realization came to her as slowly as the recognition, so that she was caught before fear could send her fleeing. And then the hawthorn branch began to get bigger. The branch grew and grew until the whole well seemed to be filled with hawthorn, and even then it didn't stop growing. The edges disappeared, but the thorn in the centre kept getting bigger

80

and bigger until that was all there was, a single enormous thorn lying on the surface of the well. It was no longer just a reflection. It was real, a deadly-looking object.

Thorny felt her hand go forward. And then Patrick's voice, blessedly normal, came out of the shadows.

"Hey, wake up! Thorny! I've been calling and calling!"

The hawthorn disappeared. Thorny blinked, feeling her hand drop to her side. She turned uncertain eyes towards Patrick. "You're too late," he said. "There was a baby fox over there. You could've seen him, if you'd come." He saw Thorny's face. "Hey, what's wrong? You look as if—" His voice changed. "Thorny! Have you see *her* again? The white lady?"

"No, no, nothing like that." Thorny strove to make her voice sound natural. "Stop staring at me! There's nothing wrong. I was just . . . daydreaming."

"If that was a daydream," he muttered, "I'll take nightmares any time."

11

Dowsing

Patrick had been cutting a willow branch when he saw the fox, and had brought the entire branch with him on his way to get Thorny. Now, a little fiercely, he began examining it for a leaf of the right size. "You're not really going to wish to see the white lady, are you?" Thorny asked him after a minute.

"You want to bet? *You* may not need to, she seems to drop in on you every five minutes, but I—"

"Patrick, I didn't see her again."

"You saw something."

"Not her." Silence. "I don't know why you want to see her, anyway. She—"

"I want to see her," he said, "because then I'll know you weren't imagining her, and you'll know you weren't imagining her, and we'll both know there really is going to be a problem on Friday night." He had selected a leaf and was leaning over the well, hands cupped. "I wish to see Thorny's white lady," he said clearly.

Thorny's breath came more quickly. A minute passed. Two. Nothing happened. Defiantly she looked at Patrick. "So I'm a mental case."

"There was no time limit on that wish," Patrick pointed out. "Anyway, even if she doesn't come, it doesn't mean you invented her. Wishes never come true here." He began stripping the leaves off the willow branch. "Thorny, what did you see in the well?"

"Nothing!"

"Have it your way." He was too proud to beg. He looked down at the Y-shaped willow switch in his hand, bare now of leaves. It gave him an idea. With Thorny looking on, frowning, he placed one hand around each of the forks, holding it so that the main branch pointed out and parallel to the ground. Yes, that was how Alec had done it. He began pacing up and down. There had to be water here to feed the well.

"What are you doing?" Thorny asked at last.

"Nothing," he said. See how *she* liked it!

"You're dowsing, aren't you?"

"If you knew, why did you ask?"

"I thought Alec said you couldn't do it." He ignored that, concentrating on what he was doing. He'd been all over the well area by this time. Surely he ought to be feeling something? "Are you dowsing for water, or for Jeremy's earth-forces?" she asked then.

"Water," he said shortly, and in case the dowsing rod wasn't sure, either, announced it clearly. "I want to find water." Nothing happened. The dowsing rod stayed motionless. He sighed.

"What's it supposed to do?" she asked.

"It'll point down when it's just over the spring. Or it should, anyway. Maybe if I try to find the earth-forces instead . . ." He stopped, rubbed the willow branch on his pants, and said loudly, "I'm trying to find earth-forces. I'm trying to find earth-forces."

He took a step or two, then waited. Nothing. Another few steps, trying different angles for the dowsing stick. Still nothing.

"Let me try," Thorny said suddenly, surprising herself as much as Patrick.

"You won't be able to do it, either," he said, handing over the stick. It was ungracious, but he couldn't help it. The white lady, Alec's medallion, Belman's curiosity, all of it was centred on Thorny. It would be a bit much if she turned out to be the dowser, too.

She took the stick gingerly, but its green springiness felt perfectly normal. She fitted her hands around the branches the way Patrick had done, then stood there a moment, feeling silly. She couldn't bring herself to talk to a stick. How could a stick find water, or anything else?

Saying nothing, but letting herself think about underground water, she took a little step towards the well. Her palms tickled. She stopped to scratch them, then took another step. The itch was worse, and her chest felt tight and hot. There was a prickliness in it, centred on Alec's medallion. She paid no more attention to Patrick. An owl hooted in the wood, and she didn't even hear.

Patrick heard it, though. He frowned. An owl, calling in daylight? He turned his head, his heart jumping when he spotted the bird. It was sitting in the vee notch of a diseased elm a stone's throw away, and it was looking right at him. It was the biggest owl he'd ever seen. Its feathers were like new snow, and its eye-rings were black as a moonless night. But most surprising, its eyes were an impossible blue. They regarded him with a cynical, knowing look that was as unfathomable as the sky, and sent chills down his spine.

Thorny was walking faster now, looking at the dowsing stick in disbelief. It wasn't just tickling, it was digging into her palms enough to hurt. It was like holding something alive and struggling. Her knuckles were white with effort, but still the twig twisted. And as it struggled with her, and she with it, Alec's medallion burned against her chest.

The owl called a second time. Patrick shivered, seeing that cruel beak opening wide, those terrible eyes glaring at him. He wanted to look away, but couldn't. He wanted to say something, but he couldn't do that, either. Thorny didn't notice. Her hands were trembling with exertion. She stared at the twig, watching it twist, seeing the pale bark strip off, feeling the circle of heat against her chest. Suddenly she couldn't deny it any longer. This was happening. It was real.

She took another step forward, suddenly eager. The pain in her chest went away. The twig responded, digging into her palms, showing her the way to water. Another step. Another. The pressure in her palms grew. The underground

84

spring was just ahead. She knew it as surely as if she could see it. The twig struggled, but she held on, suddenly exultant. "Here!" she cried triumphantly. The twig sprang from her hands. "The underground spring's right here!"

In the Circle of Awen-Un the labouring men gave a shout of satisfaction as the Keystone, securely chained, at last rose creaking at the end of the crane. A third time, terribly, the owl cried out. It was not an owl's call. It was a single long, wailing shriek, despairing, angry, defiant, a nightmare. It was the most dreadful sound Patrick had ever heard.

Thorny whirled, white-faced and staring. "What on earth was that?" she demanded, shaken. Her voice seemed loud in the silence.

Patrick shook his head, blinking at the empty elm. The owl—or whatever it had been—was not there. It hadn't flown away. It was simply gone. And he had made a wish to see Thorny's white lady. Again he shook his head, trying not to believe it. But the owl was white like the lady, and had her blue eyes, and had disappeared into thin air just as Thorny's lady had. And Jeremy had said that the moon goddess sometimes showed up as an owl. Moon goddess. He shuddered. Moon witch was more like it!

"Let's get out of here," he said.

Thorny nodded silently. But she wouldn't leave the dowsing stick. Patrick saw her bend over to pick it up, and for the first time since the business of the owl remembered his jealousy.

They stayed in the wood, but took a path that Patrick knew, leading to the northern limits of the trees. He wanted to keep under cover until they found out if Belman was still at Awen-Un. "You can't really dowse, can you?" he asked, when the wishing well was far behind.

"Actually, I can," she said, half defiantly.

"You really felt the stick move?"

"I couldn't stop it. At the end it practically jumped out of my hands." She saw his face. "Maybe it was because I had

Alec's medallion," she added, feeling sorry for him. "It got hot while I was dowsing. Maybe it helped me—"

"Can I try wearing it?" Patrick asked eagerly.

She frowned. "Alec said—" she began, then broke off. After all, Patrick had seen it already. Surely Alec's warning to keep it hidden didn't apply to him. "I suppose so," she said unwillingly.

He knew she didn't want to give it up, and that made him resentful. He held out his hand until she gave it to him. Surreptitiously he glanced at it. It still looked to him just like a thin compass, with no sign of the lights Thorny had mentioned to Alec. He slipped the chain over his head. Then, without a word, he took the dowsing stick and began concentrating harder than he ever had in his life.

"I'm looking for earth-forces," he said, firm and clear, and staring at the ground as if trying to develop x-ray vision. Nothing happened. He tried again, some distance away, still with no result. The medallion felt cool against his skin.

At last, bitterly disappointed, he gave up. "I guess Alec was right about me and dowsing," he said, handing the medallion back. "Either that or there aren't any earth-forces around here. Why don't you try to find some?"

Thorny made a face. "It's crazy trying to dowse for something when you don't even know what it is!" But she grasped the twig as she had before, adding defiantly, "Okay, I'm looking for earth-forces." And in her mind, she visualized something white and wild, like veins of electricity in the earth.

Almost at once she felt it—that strange, tickling sensation in her palms and the corresponding heat in Alec's medallion. "I'm looking for earth-forces," she said again, more eagerly this time, taking a step to the right. Nothing. To the left. The itch in her palms was back, stronger than before. She turned slightly and took another step, her heart beating faster. A shock of electricity jabbed at her. She blinked, startled. The jolt had come through the twig, not the medallion, which still bore its steady warmth. She moved forward, her eyes intent.

A short distance in front of that first jolt of power there came another, stronger this time. Patrick saw her willow rod dip as if someone had grabbed the end of it. A third time it happened, just past the second jolt. Thorny kept going forward, but nothing more happened. She turned and went back to where the last pulse of energy had occurred. Once again her rod snapped down. As if by instinct she turned and started heading north-east. Her rod stayed pointing down. Patrick saw that her hands were tense with the strain of holding it.

A pang went through him. It was so unfair! She hadn't believed in it, and he had, and who did it work for?

"Hey, watch out!" he called as Thorny almost walked into a tree near the northern edge of the wood.

She came back to her surroundings with a start. "It's a current, just like Jeremy said," she declared, her eyes shining. "It goes right under this tree. Probably past it, too."

"What about those two other places your stick went down?"

Thorny came back to him. "You think they're like streams as well?"

"Try it and see."

She found the places without difficulty, her stick dipping at what Patrick was sure were the same spots as before. "It's not a bit like when I was looking for water," she said half to herself.

"What do you mean?"

"Well, then the pull seemed to act right on the stick. But now it's more like an electric shock hitting at *me* through the stick." She turned north-east. "Look, Patrick! This is a current, too! It goes right alongside the first one."

Patrick was silent, watching. The second current went exactly parallel to the first, and so did the third. He didn't know what to say. "Well," he managed at last, "I guess you really are a dowser, and a good one. When I was helping Alec yesterday, he told me that earth-forces run in streams of three parallel lines, but that only the most powerful dowsers can detect that. Lucky beast! I don't suppose you could have invented those three lines in a million years."

"Did you think I was making it up?" Thorny demanded angrily.

"Oh, for heaven's sake, I'd have thought you'd be pleased to prove you weren't unconsciously making the twig dip."

"I suppose you're right," she said reluctantly. "Not that it'll make much difference. I don't see how my dowsing is going to be any use."

"Maybe it's one of the reasons why the moon witch got you here in the first place."

"Moon witch?" She frowned. "Oh, her. But, Patrick, it wasn't her who got me here. I came because my father said I had to. It had nothing to do with—"

"Anyway, dowsing's one reason why Alec lent you that medallion of his. I mean, he kept looking at it while he was dowsing, and you said it got hot when you dowsed. Besides, Alec said it was because I wasn't a dowser that I couldn't see that design thing on the medallion." He swallowed his pride and asked, "What does it look like, anyway?"

Thorny shook her head nervously. "Let's not talk about it here."

"Why not?"

"This is Lady Copse," she said. "If it *is* the white lady's place . . . well, maybe she shouldn't know too much about the medallion. I've got a feeling . . ." She broke off, clearly determined to say no more.

"Do you think you could still dowse without wearing it?" he asked, thinking hard.

"It didn't help *you*."

"Maybe it didn't like me. Try it, okay?"

Reluctantly she handed over the medallion again. Then she picked up her dowsing stick. Seeing her face, Patrick suddenly found himself half-wishing she could still do it. But he was as surprised as she when her stick made its first dip, then its second and third. "It still works!" she cried happily. "I *am* a dowser!"

Patrick accepted it at last. Thorny was a dowser, and he wasn't. It was as simple as that. He frowned, then shoved

88

his shoulders back. If he couldn't dowse, he still had his brains. Alec had thought enough of them to give him the job of watching out for Thorny. And however important dowsing might be, it wasn't much use if you didn't know when to use it, or why. No, there were still plenty of things to be sorted out and decided, things where he had no intention of taking a back seat. And if Thorny didn't like it, that was just too bad!

12

The Argument

Patrick was thinking hard. Thorny had dowsed one group of three earth-currents and it was heading straight for Awen-Un. It hadn't been all that difficult to find, either. Frowning, he remembered that the Lady had told Thorny Awen-Un was her major centre for controlling the earth-forces. That had been Jeremy's idea, too, and Alec's. But just exactly how major was major?

"Try another place, why don't you?" he suggested to Thorny. "And take back the medallion, okay?" Whatever it was for, she could obviously dowse without it.

A short distance from the first current Thorny found another set of three streams of earth-force heading in almost the same direction as the first. She tried again farther west, and in spite of the thick undergrowth it wasn't long before she identified four additional sets of currents, all of which headed directly for Awen-Un. "Come on, Thorny," Patrick said, grimly now. "See how many more you can find."

Thorny was getting tired, but the gravity of his voice convinced her. She asked no questions, just kept on dowsing. The afternoon wore on, growing hot even in the shadows of Lady Copse. By four o'clock she had dowsed about two dozen groups of currents, all of which headed straight for Awen-Un. "Pretty convincing, huh?" Patrick said.

Thorny slumped down at the foot of a chestnut tree. "I may be dumb, but I don't know what you're getting at," she said, running her hands wearily through her hair.

"Look, we've found twenty-plus currents of earth-force heading for Awen-Un, just from this part of Lady Copse alone. What about from all the other directions?"

Her eyes widened. "If it's the same as this everywhere," she said slowly, "there must be dozens and dozens more."

"Hundreds is more like it," he said emphatically. "And all coming together under the Circle. Thorny, Awen-Un really has to be something unusual! With all that electricity under it, it must be as live as a million-volt power transformer!"

"Then why doesn't everybody who goes near it get electrocuted?"

Patrick shook his head impatiently. "Because of the stones, of course! Alec and Jeremy must be right that they're like lightning rods. Take them away, and the charge'll build up and up, and—Thorny, we've simply got to stop Belman, or the whole of Wychwood Mount'll be fried!"

Thorny stared at him blankly, wondering what it would be like to receive a single jolt of power hundreds of times the sum of all the little ones she'd felt that day.

"But," she said, "I can't see how even a big blast of power at Awen-Un would affect the whole world. And that's what the Lady said. *A world gone mad.*"

"I want to talk to Alec," Patrick said, jumping to his feet. "He's bound to be back by now."

They made their way through the thick undergrowth to the northern edge of the trees. From here they looked across the open moor to Awen-Un. For more than two hours now the crane had been gone, taking the Keystone with it. The empty place at the south of the Circle looked raw and ugly. The sun steamed down, and in its harsh light the Circle seemed to shimmer. Just looking at it made Patrick feel queasy. Thorny reached out to lean on a branch, as if the ground beneath her feet was not quite reliable.

91

The onlookers at the Circle had dispersed, and there were only a couple of labourers left, measuring the remaining stones. But Belman was still there. Police Sergeant Quigley from Swindon was with him, listening while Belman talked.

"We're in luck," Patrick whispered. "As long as Quigley's there, Belman won't try anything. Hey, where're you going?"

"Just a sec." Thorny hurried off into the woods while Patrick waited impatiently. When she returned, her hands were full of buttercups.

"A time like this, and you have to pick flowers?" Patrick demanded incredulously.

"We don't want Belman to know what we've been doing in here," Thorny explained. "If he thinks we've been picking flowers—"

They hurried out of the woods then, keeping close together. Thorny couldn't understand why she felt so nervous. It wasn't just having to go near Belman. It was something else, something in the air. She felt almost shaky. Her hands kept wanting to reach for Alec's medallion.

Just as Patrick and Thorny reached the footpath, Belman turned and began leading his mare their way, still talking to the police officer. It was done so casually that even Patrick could not be sure it wasn't an accident. "—unreasonable," Quigley was protesting, as they came close enough to hear. "It isn't against the law to return someone's property. Not like taking it away."

"But the Keystone is no longer my property," Belman said. "It is rubbish, properly disposed of at my own expense. If someone picked up a lorry-load of rotten vegetables from the rubbish tip and dumped it on my land, wouldn't the law act on my behalf?"

The sergeant looked unhappy. "That would be different."

"I'm afraid I don't think so. There was still an act of trespass."

"We don't shoot people in England for trespassing."

The two men had stopped on the footpath, but Belman still seemed oblivious to Thorny and Patrick's approach. "I didn't ask you to shoot anybody," Belman told the sergeant gently. "I only asked for a police guard on the Circle tonight, in case the same trick is tried with the Keystone again."

"We're too short-handed to keep someone on his feet all night for something like that. You could hire your own guard, maybe."

"And if someone did bring the stone back," Belman said, "and my guard witnessed it, what would you do to the offender?"

"There is a fine for trespassing," the policeman said.

"A pound or two is hardly going to deter someone willing to go to the expense of hiring a crane." He appeared to see the two cousins then, and smiled at Thorny. But his words were still for Quigley. "Clearly if the law can do nothing, I will have to see to it myself."

"I don't know what you mean, sir," Quigley said uneasily.

"I doesn't matter." He turned to Thorny. "I see you like flowers," he said, nodding at the buttercups in Thorny's hands.

"They're for Aunt Jenny," Thorny replied, averting her eyes. "Yellow's not my colour." She flushed. What a dumb thing to say!

"You must come and see my roses," Belman said, smiling slightly. "I have one particular variety—a lovely soft peach, very much your colour, I should say—"

Thorny's flush deepened. "Mr. Belman," the policeman interjected, "you really must explain what you meant by seeing to things yourself. I do hope you don't intend to go outside the law in this. It's only a stone, after all. There's enough trouble in this village without—''

Belman ignored him. "Why not make it tomorrow?" he asked Thorny. "I could show you around the greenhouse first, and then—"

"Thorny will be busy tomorrow," Patrick said loudly.

"I think," Belman said softly, "there might be times now and then that Thorny would like to speak for herself."

It was so true that Thorny almost forgot the moment this morning when Belman's eyes had seemed terrible. She gave him a grateful look. He returned it, warm and kind. Beside her Patrick was sputtering, as was the sergeant.

"I probably will be busy," she said apologetically, "but thank you for the invitation."

Briefly Belman's face darkened. Then he laughed. "I'll send you some of the roses anyway," he replied lightly.

"She already has way more flowers than she needs," Patrick said rudely. Then he grabbed Thorny's arm and forcibly propelled her up the path.

"What's eating you?" she demanded furiously when they were out of earshot.

"I thought you were going to stay away from him?"

"I was only being polite! Which is a lot more than anybody can say for you!"

"I suppose I should be grateful you didn't actually kiss the ground he walked on."

"Don't be stupid. I told him I didn't want to see his dumb roses—"

"You wanted to say yes."

"I wanted," Thorny almost shouted, "to be allowed to make up my own mind!" And she turned on her heel and walked stiffly and proudly away.

Supper was over and the dishes were washed and put away. It had been an uncomfortable meal. Patrick and Thorny had been as polite to each other as if they were strangers. "A good night for television," Jenny suggested, hanging up her dishrag. "*The Avengers* is on. Anybody interested?"

Neither of the cousins said anything. Jenny shrugged. "Well, *I* wouldn't miss Steed and Emma Peel for anything," she announced, heading for the kitchen door.

"Not even on the third rerun?" Patrick asked, with the ghost of a wink at Thorny. She wasn't sure if she'd seen it or only imagined it.

"Not even then," his mother said. "Put the kettle on, will you, Thorny? I need another cup of tea."

"Well," Patrick said uncomfortably. Thorny had her back to him and was filling the kettle. Carefully she put it on the range. "I'll light it," he offered, getting out the matches.

"Okay," Thorny said coolly.

There was a long silence. Off in the lounge the television rang with gunfire. "Stupid series," Patrick said. "Fifty people killed in each show. Dumb."

"I like it," Thorny said.

Patrick grinned shamefacedly. "So do I."

"About this afternoon—" Thorny began.

Patrick interrupted her. "It was just Belman, Thorny. The way he was sucking up to you made me see red. You weren't doing anything wrong, not really, but I was so sure you wanted to . . . . Anyway, I didn't mean to push you around." It was the closest he could come to an apology.

After a moment she said, "Maybe I'm just that kind of person. The kind other people push around, I mean."

Patrick's brows went up. After a moment she went on. "What happened when you talked with Alec?" She had come straight back to the cottage after the argument, and had been wondering ever since what Alec had told Patrick.

"I never saw him," her cousin replied shortly. "I waited around for him as long as I could, but he still hasn't come back." He rubbed his forehead.

"Well," Thorny said slowly, "he never did say he was coming back today."

"But Tom Avery's held his room for him because Alec said he'd be needing it. And his things are all still there."

"Maybe he'll be back later tonight," Thorny suggested, tugging at her ear. After all, Alec might have had any number of errands to hold him up.

But all the rest of the evening, while they made themselves sit still in front of *On the Buses* and a disaster-filled local news program, the niggling worry about Alec never quite left them. "He's bound to be back in the morning," Thorny whispered reassuringly as they said goodnight.

"Is he?" Patrick replied. "I'm not so sure."

13

A Shot in the Dark

The cottage was asleep. A web of moonlight hung between the chimneys and over the thatched eaves, looping across Jenny's vegetable garden to catch the motionless trees in a silver net. Away behind the weeping willow Stratton Hall was a hushed shadow. Farther still, a single shaft from the descending moon skimmed the lilypond in the park and reached out to the gaudy stone statues of the zodiac. It was a silent night. There was no wind, no barking dog, no restless murmur in the middle of sleep. In all of Wychwood Mount only three people were awake.

One was trudging along the moonlit footpath with camera and a surveying theodolite. The second was at Awen-Un, unmoving and unmoved. The third was sitting in the big ivory-backed chair that Sir George Stratton had loved, motionless in the firelight. Only now and then did his eyes flicker to the window where the curtains were shut fast against the moonlight and the dark. A few hours till dawn, that was all. He waited for it, for another furnace of a day.

In Aunt Jenny's cottage Thorny lay still in her bed in a ribbon of moonlight. She was dreaming. She was on a boat in the middle of a wide blue sea, alone, the tiller in her hand, happy. And then came wind, cold, stinking as the grave. She was at sea still, but no longer alone. People, a plague of people! She could not escape them. They sought her out, spoke to her, gave her things, laughed when she refused. And still the flowers came, peach-coloured roses and yellow ones and orchids like spiders; and bundles of hawthorn, dagger-barbed. Each flower was a message requiring her allegiance to a different cause, and each one, dreadfully, received it. *It was for that world that thou wert created.* For that world, and this. For every world but her own.

And the ship faded, and the ocean, and she saw then that there was only one world, after all. It was a two-coloured ball, dark on one side, light on the other, yet everywhere it was lit from within by the threads of its energy. Nerves, those great white roots, twined and connected, fibre to fibre, branch to branch, passing on life and collecting it: the carriers of the force that kept the world alive. The earth-force.

In her sleep Thorny moaned, feeling once again those jolting bursts of energy through her dowsing stick. Nerves. She had dowsed nerves. And the brain? The nerve centre of the world? Where was it? She moaned again, knowing. Awen-Un. The loom of all cloth, the pattern-maker: twelve stones weaving, twelve stones that made the world breathe. Destroy the brain, and what is left? Cold, wild, electric death, the limbs that jerk when the frog is gone, the shark that bites when dead. And now Awen-Un was a brain without its cortex. Did it know? She thought it did. And in her dream Thorny wept.

You can stop it. You must! Come. Come to me now!

And she saw a speck of red glowing amid the stones of Awen-Un, the only bit of colour in all that moon-bleached world. And then the moon faded, and the speck of red grew to a screaming mouth in a face she knew, and with it a body gushing blood. And she heard a gunshot echo and re-echo, blending with the scream.

Thorny's eyes flew open, wide with the horror of her dream. Quickly she got out of bed, throwing on some clothes, fumbling for her shoes. She had to go to the Circle, at once. And she had to go alone.

The wind was rising. Moving bars of shadow lay like a convict's shirt on the village, alternating with the silver-grey dust of moonlight. It was an eerie night. Thorny could feel the wind fingering her face, exploring her nostrils with its damp-earth smell. Away behind the White Horse the nearly full moon was low in the sky. Only now and then was it completely visible, more often half-veiled by the tatters of blowing clouds. There were no lights on in the village. The houses were deep patches of shadow in the night, or moon-spattered grey and unreal. The night was full of their restless sounds, shutters rattling, doors clicking in and out, trees scratching against window-panes.

Thorny hurried on to the footpath. She was afraid to slow down, and even more afraid to think. Over and over again she wished she had never come to Wychwood Mount. Faster and faster she hurried until she was almost running. High in the sky a white owl circled the moor.

She was only a short distance from Awen-Un when a hand came out from behind and clutched her arm. Panting with terror, she whirled to face her attacker. The moon was behind a cloud.

"Let go of me! Let go!"

She almost cried with relief when Patrick's familiar voice replied, "Not till you tell me what you're doing."

"Patrick!"

"I asked you what you were doing."

Relief turned to anger. "Taking a stroll, what does it look like?"

"I thought you trusted me," Patrick said, his hand gripping her even tighter. "I thought we were in this together. But the first chance you get it's off to the Circle, sneaking away and leaving me out—"

"There's somebody out there dying!" Thorny cried out. His grip slackened, and Thorny wrenched herself free. "I dreamed it!" she half-shouted at him. "That's why I'm here!" And with a gulping sob she threw herself back down the path, running like a hunted animal.

He was after her at once. Someone dying. God. She had dreamed it. But people had nightmares all the time. Why should it have sent Thorny pounding down to Awen-Un in the middle of the night?

Without slowing down Patrick dug out his pocket flashlight. But Thorny didn't seem to need light. She knew when to leave the footpath, though the stones of Awen-Un were only shadows. Heedlessly she pounded across the broken ground, heading directly for the most westerly stone. And then she stopped. And that was when Patrick saw the shapeless lump sprawled out like an oversized rag-doll on the ground beside her.

It was Jeremy Kingsley.

"Oh, my God," Patrick said.

"Is he . . . dead?"

She was in the way, kneeling in a pool of Jeremy's blood.

"Get back," Patrick ordered. He felt for Jeremy's wrist, trying not to think about the awful hole in his chest. The pulse was weak, but it was there. "He's still alive, but if he bleeds any more . . . Do you have a clean handkerchief? Something we can use as a bandage?"

"Take my jacket."

It was one of those brushed cotton things, highly absorbent. She stripped it off quickly. Patrick bunched it up and pressed it to the wound in Jeremy's chest while Thorny held the light. Her jacket grew wet at once.

"We've got to get help," Patrick grunted. "Do you know which house is Dr. Wilder's?"

The light wavered, glancing on Jeremy's broken camera, some other kind of equipment, and a little farther to hover on something small and ugly and metallic. The gun. At least that meant that whoever had tried to kill Jeremy wasn't still hanging around waiting to shoot someone else.

"Is Wilders' the cottage with the green door?" Thorny got out then, returning the light to Jeremy's face.

"No. It'd take too long to explain. I'll have to be the one to go. You'll be all right," he told her. "One of us has to stay. If he loses any more blood—"

"I know."

"Just keep pressing on the bandage." She said nothing. "I'll be back as soon as I can, I promise. You can keep the light."

Patrick was gone the moment she nodded. He didn't like leaving the two of them alone, but if Jeremy didn't get help soon, he would die. Fifteen minutes to Dr. Wilder's, he calculated, thudding along the footpath, ten to get him up and to ring for an ambulance and the police, fifteen more to get back. With luck Thorny and Jeremy would be alone for only forty minutes.

Alone, Thorny held on to the bandage as tightly as her trembling right hand allowed. Jeremy was so still! Could he have died without her knowing? She wanted to feel for his pulse, but her right hand was busy, and her left seemed to be glued to the flashlight. She shuddered, and the stones of Awen-Un shuddered with her.

Time passed. She marked it by the moon. It had been low in the sky when Patrick had left, and now it was lower still, almost on the horizon. The wind was blowing away the clouds that had hidden it. Silver and bright and satisfied as a cat, it perched on the western hills, waiting. She turned her eyes away from it. But now and then, like a magnet, the beam of her flashlight shone towards the gun.

Silence, utter and complete; the natural world in limbo. Thorny quivered, suddenly aware. It was then that Awen-Un began to weep.

She didn't move, she didn't think. She might have been stone herself. What was left of Awen-Un keened, grieved and hungry and out of control: eleven stones, in need and knowing it. And the earth trembled, feeling its danger. A humming sound filled the air, high and intense, rising and falling. Jeremy twitched with pain, but Thorny didn't see. In the southwest the moon sat on the horizon, a huge, flattened, gleaming ball. A path of silver light was laid before it, unrolling like a carpet towards the Circle of Awen-Un, blanching the tip of one of the stones and going on from it

101

across the Circle, coming at last to a halt at the southern edge where the Keystone ought to have been. And though the Keystone wasn't there, the Moon Witch was.

Moonlight and pure steel, surrounded by her grieving stones, the goddess touched her hand to the Keystone's empty socket. And then, slowly, she began to move. Where she touched she left light, where she breathed the air quietened, where she moved the ground became solid and firm. She wove a path through the Circle, and behind her she left pattern and order. And for her, the mother of the world, the grieving of the stones sank to a low hum and lower, and then at last there was silence.

Thorny bowed her head, tears pricking her eyes at the beauty she had seen. It was then that the lady came to her. Slowly, shudderingly, Thorny raised her eyes. Not one person after all, but three, all separate, all different, yet all the same. The mother, the young girl, the hag: purity turned wanton; selflessness made greedy; and the hag with her wrinkled face and unpretending, all-consuming eyes. *I am waiting for thee*, that face said. *Avoid me how thou will, thou wilt come.*

"No!" Thorny cried.

We made thee. Thou art ours. Thou wilt do all that we require of thee.

"I won't!"

For the sake of the earth, for order and pattern, for the rightness of life. For thine own sake, Hawthorn, for freedom, for revenge!

The wrinkled lips smiling, sure of her, waiting. Pick up the gun. *We will tell thee what to do.*

14

The Hero

"If this is some kind of joke, young Patrick—"

The threat was from Mr. Robson, and it wasn't the first. Patrick gritted his teeth. "Can't you tell when somebody's serious? I've told you and told you—"

Pudgy little Dr. Wilder, marching along at the other end of the stretcher, said, "Yes, and we listened to you, too. We've roused up Aggie Millson, which means your mother is pacing the floor. We've got half the Swindon police department on its way, and the ambulance, too. And we're lugging this stretcher through the wilderness in the pitch dark all because we listened to you. And all I have to say is, there just better be a wounded man at the other end, or there'll be the devil to pay."

"If you don't go a little faster," Patrick said through his teeth, "there'll be a dead man there."

It had been more than an hour since he'd left Thorny. His original calculations hadn't accounted for the need for a stretcher, or having to rouse up another household to get someone to help carry it. He hadn't anticipated the trials of explaining things to Mrs. Millson at the telephone exchange, either, or the slowness of the Swindon police at three in the morning. And now, to have to make his way back to Awen-Un at the snail's pace of Mr. Robson and Dr. Wilder . . . !

"I don't see why I can't go on ahead," he complained for

about the fifth time since they had started. "Doesn't it bother you that Thorny has been alone with a dying man for over an hour?"

"Your being on the loose isn't going to change that," the doctor said. "And in case you've forgotten, there's a would-be murderer out here somewhere. Your mother would never forgive me if he started taking pot-shots at you, too."

"He left his gun behind. I told you."

"He could have any number of others."

"Then what's to stop him shooting us all?"

"Belt up, Patrick," Mr. Robson growled. "We're going to keep an eye on you, and that's flat."

"Barn door," Patrick muttered. But his anger faded, overtaken by weariness and fear and the tick-tick-tick of his brain thinking. What had Jeremy been doing at Awen-Un? Who had shot him? And why? And why, above all things, had Thorny dreamed about it?

A sudden memory made him clap his hand to his head. "Belman!" he exclaimed.

"What about him?" the doctor said sharply.

The words tumbled out. "He was thinking of putting his own guard on the Circle tonight in case the Keystone came back—in case someone brought it back again, I mean. He said something about taking care of it himself. You don't suppose he—?"

"Shot Kingsley, thinking he was bringing back the stone?" Mr. Robson said.

"Not our Belman," Dr. Wilder disagreed sourly. "He's not the kind to do his own dirty work."

"Maybe that man Red—" Patrick suggested.

"You have to be either awfully stupid or awfully bloodthirsty to kill a man for someone else," the doctor said quellingly. "That Red bloke doesn't seem to me to be either."

104

After that they were silent. Patrick was remembering Jeremy saying he wanted to get the Circle surveyed. But he hadn't been able to. The men had been working on it all day, and wouldn't let anyone near. What if Jeremy had decided to take his survey tonight, in the moonlight? That would explain his camera, anyway, and maybe that other funny-looking instrument as well. Suppose he had waltzed out here in the moonlight, and Belman had been waiting: Belman who had already decided it was Kingsley who had brought the Keystone back the first time. Would Belman really have shot him? Patrick shivered at the thought.

In the hour since he'd been out on the moor, things had changed. The clouds had fled, leaving the sky a pin-cushion of stars. The gibbous moon had set. The wind was not as strong as before, nor as cool, but it had a faint odour, like rot. Faster Patrick walked, and faster. His legs had taken on a life of their own, and he couldn't stop them. Deaf to Dr. Wilder's shouts, he began to run, speeding up the slope that overlooked the Circle.

"Thorny!" he called, a hoarse croak, uncertain. There was no reply. Behind him he could hear Mr. Robson cursing steadily, and Dr. Wilder's walrus puffs.

He ran down the slope and into the Circle, counting the stones. " . . . nine, ten, eleven," he counted. The lump that was Jeremy was lying still and alone against the tenth. Then, leadenly, "Twelve." He wasn't even surprised. The Keystone was back again. In the hour that had passed since his leaving, the Keystone had come back.

Thorny was behind the Keystone, sitting with her back to it. Her eyes were open, but she didn't blink, not even when Patrick shone the light right in them. "Thorny, are you all right?" He had hold of her shoulders and was shaking them hard. She looked at him then, a dazed look, as if she were

105

seeing right through him to the shadows beyond. "Dr. Wilder, quick!" Patrick shouted, hearing the two men come stumbling into the Circle. "There's something wrong with Thorny!"

"Where's Kingsley? Devil take you, Patrick, I can't see a thing!"

Patrick ran the lantern over to him. "Thorny's over there by the Keystone—"

"The Keystone!" Mr. Robson exclaimed. "But—"

"Your cousin's not been shot, too?" the doctor demanded.

"No, but she's strange, She—"

"Then let me see to Kingsley."

By the light of the lantern his examination of the wounded man was thorough and swift. The wound had stopped bleeding, but the doctor's fingers disturbed it, and the blood started trickling again. "Antiseptic," the doctor said shortly. Mr. Robson handed it to him. "Better get this part over with while he's still unconscious." Silence, Patrick wincing. "Right, that ought to do it. Now for some bandages. Good man, Robson. And I'll need my syringe." He poked through his bag. Thorny came up then, ghostlike in the lantern-light. Dr. Wilder looked at her swiftly. "You've had a shock, my girl," he said, brusque but kind. "Sit down. Patrick, you, too."

"Jeremy's not going to . . . die, is he?" Patrick almost choked on the words.

"No. Not this time. Strong as a carthorse, this chap is. But he can thank his fates you two were out here tonight. No, I don't want to hear why. Save it for your mother. Robson, give me a hand strapping him into the stretcher, will you?"

"Should we get the gun?" Patrick asked hesitantly. "The police will want to see it, won't they?"

"Not your business," Dr. Wilder said. "They'll get it in the morning."

106

"But it's just over there." And he pointed the lantern to where he had last seen it, cold and small and ugly.

But the gun was gone.

"Thorny!" he said. "What happened to the gun?"

"Gun?" Thorny said, her voice low and drugged-sounding. "What gun?"

"The gun that was here! You must have seen—"

But Thorny only shook her head. "I don't know what you're talking about."

"No, you don't, young man!" Firmly Jenny grabbed the hand Patrick had raised to knock on Thorny's door. It was two in the afternoon, and Patrick had been awake since noon. Thorny had been asleep for nine hours straight.

"She doesn't need to sleep forever," he told his mother as loudly as he dared.

"Shh!" Jenny drew him away. When they were in the kitchen and the door was closed, she turned on him. "The doctor said to let her sleep, and I won't have you waking her! I wish you were snoring in your bed, too, instead of mooning around the place like a discontented cow."

"What else is there to do?" he said crossly. "You won't let me go out, you won't let me talk to Thorny, you won't even let me use the phone—"

"I should have thought you'd done enough last night to last you a lifetime."

Jenny had been standing at the door waiting for them when they got back from the Circle just before five that morning. She'd been so relieved to see them both in one piece that she'd hardly said a word, just shoved them into bed with a hot water bottle apiece and a severe warning not to get up until at least noon. Today had been a different story, however.

"You're not starting in on that again, are you?" Patrick groaned.

"I still don't understand why you followed Thorny," Jenny said, tying some string around a box of cakes. "Why didn't you stop her, or at least ask what she was up to?"

"I had to catch her first, didn't I? Anyway, if I'd stopped her, Jeremy might have bled to death. Doesn't it matter to you that we probably saved his life?" Jeremy was out of danger now, Jenny had told him, though the bullet had come very close to his heart.

"Of course it matters. I'm very glad of it. I just wish it could have happened some other way. Do you realize how close you came to witnessing an attempted murder? And that gun disappearing like that! The police are still looking for it, but if they don't find it, and you didn't imagine it—"

"I didn't imagine it," he said coldly.

"Well, then, someone must have taken it away. The murderer, I suppose, worrying about fingerprints. And that's what sends chills down my spine. Because he must have crept back to the Circle when Thorny was looking after your Mr. Kingsley. What if she had seen him?"

"Well, she didn't," Patrick said. "She didn't even see the gun, she said."

"Lucky for her," Jenny said darkly. She put the cake box by the door.

"Are you going out?" Patrick asked hopefully.

"*I* am," she replied meaningly. "The hospital auxiliary meeting, remember? Now where's my handbag gotten to this time?"

Nothing more about him having to stay in, anyway, Patrick told himself. "I don't suppose for a minute you're intending to stay indoors," Jenny said, reading his mind.

He flushed guiltily. "It's just not fair," he said defiantly. "Everybody in the village knows more than I do about the Keystone and the police and the gun and everything. Who was it who did the rescuing, anyway?"

His mother sighed. "I suppose if you go out it'll keep you from bothering Thorny," she said. "Oh, all right. Get out of here. But stay away from reporters. And whatever you do, you're not, definitely not, to go to the Circle!"

Patrick was gone before she could change her mind. He headed at once for the White Horse. All morning he'd tried to get a chance at the telephone, so he could find out if Alec was back yet. He had to be, by now. Or at least there must have been some word from him!

June Avery met Patrick on the doorstep, her shopping basket over her arm. "Hullo," she said cheerfully. "We've been wondering when you were going to show up. All slept out, are you, after last night?"

"Is Alec Underwood back yet, Mrs. Avery?" he asked anxiously.

Her brows rose in surprise. "Mr. Underwood? No, not yet. No news of him, either. But we're holding his room as long as we can. Why?"

"I just wanted to talk to him," Patrick said evasively.

She left then. Aimlessly, Patrick drifted into the inn. Alec wasn't back. His things were all here, and he'd made no mention of intending to stay away more than a few hours, and there'd been no phone call since to explain. Where was he?

Tom Avery was polishing glasses behind the bar of the public. He was a paunchy, growly-voiced man with kind eyes. "All alone?" he asked in mock amazement. "Those newspaper blokes are going to kick themselves, wasting time on the Keystone and the police, with a genuine hero here going begging. Lemonade?" He was already pouring it.

"Thanks," Patrick said uncomfortably.

"You look a bit droopy. Not enough sleep, or did Jenny kick up rough?"

"She was okay," Patrick shrugged.

"Your Mr. Kingsley is a lucky man," Tom went on. "You and your cousin coming along when you did, I mean. Saved his life." He poured himself a lemonade, too, and drank it all in one gulp. "Everybody would really like to know what Kingsley was doing out there in the first place," he went on curiously. "Was he bringing the Keystone back, or what?"

"The Keystone wasn't anywhere near when Thorny and I found him," Patrick said. "But yesterday he told us he wanted to survey Awen-Un, before Belman got rid of it altogether. *Is* Belman working on the Circle again?"

"He's got his work-crew hanging around waiting for the police to give the okay. They've got the whole area cordoned off. Searching for clues, people say. I'm guessing you'll see more than you want of them before this is over. That goes for that young cousin of yours, too. They say," he added thoughtfully, "that it was some kind of a vision that took her out in the night, and you after her. I suppose she saw—"

He broke off as Margie Taylor came into the public. She was a spotty-faced girl with a big stomach and a mouth to match. "Well, and have you put all the fresh linen out?" Tom growled at her.

"All but Rooms Nine and Eleven," she said, smirking at Patrick. "No keys."

"Have you lost those blessed keys again?"

"Can't help it if guests go away with them, can I? Anyway, Eleven's just a reporter, an' Nine's Mr. Underwood, an' his linen was fresh yesterday."

"In this inn," Tom said exasperatedly, "linen is changed every day. Got me?" He threw a set of keys at Margie. "Now get to it, my girl. Leave the doors unlocked so I can have a look afterwards."

"I'll have you know I don't like being checked up on," the girl said, tossing her head. "I know my job, thank you very much."

"Then do it," Mr. Avery said, and she flounced out.

"Didn't Alec Underwood even phone?" Patrick asked, not very hopefully.

"Not a word. If he's not back soon, I'll have to store his things. We're being plagued with room requests now that the papers have got wind of the Keystone coming back again, and the shooting. Ah, well, nobody can say it's not good for business. You off?"

"I guess so. Thanks for the lemonade." Patrick was doing his best to appear aimless. But when he was out the door of the public and into the main hall of the inn he made directly for the stairs. Room Nine. Unlocked and waiting for him, once Margie was finished. It couldn't be illegal to go into an unlocked room, could it? Well, even if it was, he had no choice. He had to have a look at Alec's things before Tom jumbled them all together and destroyed any clues there might be to Alec's disappearance. For it *was* a disappearance, Patrick was now certain. Something had gone badly wrong with Alec's plans. And Patrick was determined to find out what.

15

Greaser

What Patrick hoped to find was the sort of thing spies always came across on television. A piece of blotting paper with a word written backwards on it, maybe; a notepad with the top sheet gone but its impression carried through; possibly an appointment book with initials and addresses, or a cryptic telephone message crumpled in the wastepaper basket. He found nothing of the kind. Margie had left the room fairly clean, and Alec himself was obviously too tidy for his own good. Shirts and ties and underwear were folded neatly in the bureau, an extra jacket was hung in the massive old wardrobe, and the solitary suitcase was stowed out of the way in a corner. The suitcase was just a suitcase, with no obvious false bottom, and there was nothing under the mattress.

Patrick was fumbling among the shaving gear and brushes when he heard noises in the hall outside. He froze, listening. Tom couldn't be checking up on Margie already, could he? But that was his voice—and another man's. They were coming in!

He didn't know how he managed to get himself squeezed into the tiny space behind the angled wardrobe before the two men came in. He couldn't see the men from this angle, but he could hear them.

" . . . just as well," Tom was saying. "We'll be needing his room, and I'm glad not to have to store his things."

"I'll be getting to it, then," the stranger said—a big city voice, undereducated, but with a chilling kind of competence

Patrick didn't like. "Thanks for showing me up," he added. "I'm sure you've your own business to take care of."

Tom moved farther into the room, planting himself where Patrick could just see his narrowed eyes. The other man said nothing, but from the thuds and grunts it was apparent he was already at work. What was this stranger doing with Alec's things? And why was Tom allowing it?

"I doubt if you really need to crawl under that bed," Tom said after a moment. "Mr. Underwood seems to have been a tidy sort."

"Things get lost," said the stranger. "Really, landlord, you needn't stay. I'll see you afterwards to settle Mr. Underwood's bill."

"Nothing much to settle," Tom said, looking at him oddly. "He paid in advance for room and meals, and paid for his drinks as he had them. Didn't he tell you?"

"I meant," the man said smoothly, "for his telephone calls."

"Yes, well, I suppose he might have made some. He's in Oxford, you say?"

"I can give you a telephone number," the stranger said, an edge to his voice. "If you want to check it out."

"No, no, that's all right. You had that note from Mr. Underwood authorizing you to collect his things. Nice for him, running into old friends like that. Will he be staying with them long?"

Staying with friends! Soaked with sweat, crammed between the wardrobe and the wall, Patrick wanted to shout his disbelief aloud. Alec, going away on a casual visit, when he'd been dead worried leaving, when he'd promised Thorny and Patrick an explanation about the white lady, when he'd left Thorny his medallion? Two days gone, and no word, not even a telephone call, and now this stranger shows up? No way! Patrick thought violently. How could Tom believe it?

There came the sound of bedding being shaken out, then the visible jab of a ringed hand sliding professionally into the cracks of the armchair near the wardrobe. Then over to

113

the bureau, just the edge of his back coming into Patrick's line of sight. For quite a while there was only the noise of drawers being opened and shut, of things being dumped into a suitcase. Patrick was in an agony of pins and needles, but he was scared, too, more scared than he wanted to admit. What had happened to Alec?

"Excuse me," the stranger said to Tom, a forced courtesy, and Tom moved aside to allow him access to the wardrobe. There was the sound of doors opening and shutting, the jangle of coat hangers, a muffled curse as the man felt in Alec's empty pockets.

"I think you must've got everything Underwood ever owned, by this time. Or would you like me to fetch a saw, so you can take the wardrobe apart, just in case?" Tom's voice was heavy with sarcasm.

"Mr. Underwood asked me specially to look out for a compass—sort of a medallion—he'd left here. Means a lot to him, that compass. Antique, something like that. I've been looking for it."

Patrick was chewing on his lip so hard it almost bled. The medallion! That was the lie that proved everything else was a lie, too. Alec knew where he'd left the medallion. Which meant—

"We'll send it on to him if we find it," Tom said. "You can give me the address."

And then, at last, the man turned so he was in Patrick's view. Furrowed, greasy face, eyes narrow as a ferret, black hair shiny with oil . . . Patrick swallowed. It was the man with the potato peelings: Belman's second servant, the one who kept indoors and out of people's sight. Belman had sent him here with a fake story to keep people from looking for Alec.

And clearly he wanted the medallion, too. Maybe more than anything, Belman wanted the medallion.

"Alec's not dead," Thorny said. They were sitting on the grass behind the cottage, staring towards the domed roof of

114

Stratton Hall. It was five in the afternoon. They had been talking for almost an hour. "I know he's not dead." Her hand went to her chest, to the place where the medallion rested.

"And does the medallion know *where* he is, too?" Patrick interpreted.

"Near," she said. She jerked her head towards the Hall. "There, probably."

"God. The Hall's like a fortress since he changed all the locks. Thorny, I think we're going to have to go to the police."

"Why should they believe us? We don't have any proof that Alec's even disappeared, let alone that Belman's got him."

"I could identify Greaser. That servant of Belman's, I mean."

"Not without admitting that you were hiding in Alec's room the whole time. And, anyway, even if you got the police to listen, and they went over to the Hall with you, what makes you think that Greaser guy would show himself? He's been hiding out all this time, you said. Why would he come to the door and say hello? They'd have to search for him, and I can't see them getting a search warrant or whatever they do over here, just because you said he'd kidnapped Alec."

"I see what you mean," Patrick said gloomily. A long moment passed. He squared his shoulders. "We're just going to have to rescue Alec ourselves."

She rubbed her forehead wearily. "Sure, James Bond, why not?"

He flushed angrily. "Fine. You think of something, if my ideas are all so bad."

Thorny's tired face grew even more pinched and white. "I don't know," she said, her voice low and miserable. "I can't think. I can't even remember things. And it's already Thursday."

He had to ask it. "Thorny, what really happened last night?"
A long moment passed. Very gently, he said, "You do remember some of it, don't you?"

She waited so long he didn't think she was going to answer.
Then, with a sigh that was half a sob, she said, "I saw her."

"The white lady?"

"It was awful." Thorny shuddered. And then it all came
out. The crying of the stones, the coming of the Moon Witch,
the amazing thing the Moon Witch had done to make the
Circle well again, the dreadful moment she had turned into
three. "They wanted me to take the gun," she whispered.

"Why?"

"I don't know." She tugged at her ear, hard. "I just don't
know."

"Did you take it?"

"I didn't want to."

"But did you anyway?"

"That's just it. I can't remember!"

"You don't remember? How could you forget something
like that?"

"I don't know! Don't you think I've asked myself and
asked myself?"

"But you do remember everything else?"

"I didn't at first. When you came back with the stretcher,
I couldn't remember anything at all, but it's been coming
back to me." She looked down, and Patrick knew she was
trying not to cry.

"I guess you couldn't have taken the gun," he said. "We'd
have seen it. And if you'd hidden it, the police would have
found it. They searched the whole area with a fine-toothed
comb."

"*Somebody* must have taken it," she said dully.

"What about the Moon Witch?"

"If she'd wanted it, why would she have bothered asking
me to take it?"

Patrick was silent. She was right. It didn't make sense.
But the only other possibility was that the man who'd shot

Jeremy had come back to fetch his gun, and somehow Patrick couldn't believe that either. Not with the Moon Witch there. "What happened then?" he asked. "Do you remember?" She turned wild eyes towards him, shaking her head violently. "You do remember," he said sternly.

"No. It's too horrible."

"It was the Keystone, wasn't it? You saw it come back. Thorny! It came by itself, didn't it? Didn't it?"

She covered her face with her hands and sobbed.

16

The Telephone Call

Dinner was a tense meal. Jenny had visited Jeremy Kingsley after her meeting, but not even the news that he sent them his love and gratitude could lighten the two cousins' mood. After dinner a police inspector came and asked them a lot of questions. It was hard to answer him without saying anything about the Moon Witch, but they tried. He left, frowning, and they were so dispirited that they didn't even argue when Jenny ordered them to bed. Shrugging into his pajamas, Patrick stared out his window at the almost full moon. One day until the eclipse, he thought, and here they were, going to bed. There didn't seem to be anything else they could do.

The telephone rang just as Thorny was getting into bed. Patrick stuck his head around the door to Thorny's room.

"I think it's your father!" he hissed.

"Has Miriam tried Dramamine?" Jenny was saying as Thorny, barefoot and heart thumping, appeared at her side. A long spate of words answered her. " Well, I'm sorry," Jenny put in, "but it's not a major catastrophe, is it? Actually, John, I'm glad you rang. We've been having quite a time here. Last night Thorny and Patrick—" Pause. "I do think you ought to know. Thorny and Patrick saved a man's life last night. A shooting." Annoyed. "Yes, in Wychwood Mount! Yes, yes, she's quite all right. She—" John's voice took over then. Thorny and Patrick crowded nearer, trying to hear.

"And Miriam?" Jenny said at last. "How does she feel about this idea of yours? It is her honeymoon, too, you know." Long silence. "Well, I don't think Thorny's having as bad a time as all that, but if you were going to ask her anyway, I'll put her on." And she turned to her niece, holding out the receiver.

"Hello, Dad," Thorny said, her colour high.

"Hello, Pet. What's this I hear about you playing heroine? And in Wychwood Mount of all places!"

His voice was light, almost amused. Reaching for the phone, Thorny had been ready to pour the whole story out to him, but now she didn't know what to say. "It wasn't a big deal," she got out at last. "We were just in the right place at the right time."

"You're all right? No bullet-holes in your best jeans?"

"No, I—"

"Well, you'll have to tell me all about it when we're together. That's really why I'm calling. I've been thinking, Thorny. How would you like to join Miriam and me when our boat docks in Athens on Saturday?"

Thorny's thoughts were spinning. "Saturday? You mean the day after tomorrow? But I thought I was supposed to stay here for the whole summer!"

"You make it sound like a prison term," her father said, a smile in his voice. "Has it really been that bad?" But before she could say anything, John McCall went on. "You'll love Egypt, Thorny. We'll keep with the cruise until Cairo, then take a smaller ship down the Nile, visiting the pyramids on the way. Even Miriam should be able to manage that—"

"Won't she mind," Thorny asked, "me butting in on her honeymoon?"

"It's not turning out to be much of a honeymoon," her father said. "Miriam's been dreadfully seasick. Poor girl," he added.

Thorny was silent. She was thinking about the three suit-cases full of new clothes Miriam had bought especially for the cruise. Gorgeous, fashionable Miriam, who would sooner be seen dead than vomiting . . . "Why couldn't you just cancel the rest of the cruise and go somewhere else?"

"I'm sure Miriam wouldn't want that. She feels guilty enough as it is. Frankly, she has been a bit of a fool about this whole thing. It turns out that she's always had a problem with motion sickness, but didn't want to tell me."

Thorny remembered the day her father had brought home the cruise brochures, how pleased he had been that there were vacancies at the right time, how he'd gone on and on about it being the trip of a lifetime. Miriam had been pretty quiet. Poor Miriam. "Why don't you just surprise her with it, Dad, and cancel the cruise on your own?" Thorny said tentatively.

For a brief moment she thought her father was going to be angry. Then, mildly, he said, "I thought you'd have wanted to see the pyramids with me. Didn't you always say you'd like to?"

"Yes, but—"

"And it's not as if you can be enjoying yourself where you are."

No, she wasn't enjoying herself. How could she be, with everything that was happening? But if it had just been Aunt Jenny and Patrick, she realized suddenly, if it had just been Wychwood Mount with its church bells and evenings of Scrabble and *The Avengers* and tea, she would have enjoyed it very much.

"I like Aunt Jenny and Patrick, Dad," she said aloud, stiff and unhappy.

"I've already booked your flight, Thorny. You leave to-morrow at six from Heathrow."

Tomorrow at six. But tomorrow night was the eclipse. And even if all she did was stand there and watch, she had to stay. "I can't come tomorrow, Dad."

"I beg your pardon?" Silence. "Thorny? Are you there?"

"Yes, I'm here."

"It has to be tomorrow," her father said impatiently. "There's no other way you can make connection with our ship. So stop being a silly girl. Write this down: British Airways Flight 270 —"

"Dad, I can't come."

"You don't really want me to have to tour the Greek Islands on my own, do you?" There was an edge to his voice that Thorny had never heard before.

"I'm . . . sorry," she whispered. "I can't help it."

"I see. Well." He was cool now. "Well, I won't say you haven't surprised me. I thought you would hate Wychwood Mount—"

So why did you send me here, then, Thorny thought miserably.

"—but it seems you have more of your mother in you than I thought. And since you like it so much, I have a proposition for you. Why not stay on a bit longer?"

"Please don't—" Thorny began, but her father went on as if he didn't even hear.

"British schools are excellent, better than most Canadian ones. Funnily enough, Miriam and I had been discussing your education, anyway. We'd been thinking a boarding school might be just what you need. Make some new friends, give you some confidence, make you independent, that sort of thing. You could visit us in the holidays, when I'm not away on business—"

"Dad!"

"—and you'll be wanting to go off to university anyway fairly soon—"

"Dad, please. I didn't mean to—"

His voice was friendly now, even pleased. "No need to get upset, Thorny. It's not because you wouldn't agree to fly

121

out. It's just given us both the opportunity, you see? Now be a good girl and put your aunt on the phone. Jenny will be needing money. There'll be your fees, and uniforms, and a dollar or two to feed you with—"

But Thorny had dropped the receiver and run from the room.

"If it's any comfort to you," Jenny said gently, "he probably did intend to send you away to school, anyway. Even if you'd dropped everything and flown to Athens when he asked—"

She sat down on Thorny's bed, not touching her, just talking in that gentle, matter-of-fact voice. Thorny listened dully, her face in her pillow. She had stopped crying. Dad had never liked cry-babies.

"Actually, I should be proud, if I were you," Jenny said almost casually.

"Proud?" Thorny demanded bitterly, half sitting up. "What did I do that was so great?"

"You didn't bow down to him. You showed him you were a person. You broke free of him, Thorny, and you did it even though you still love him. That's better than the rest of us."

"The rest of us?"

"Here, have some tea." Jenny handed her a cup. "Yes, the rest of us. Me. Your mother. Others, too. Everybody John McCall dominates just that little bit too long."

"I don't know what you mean," Thorny said, flat and empty.

"He can't help it," Jenny said. "It's not something he does on purpose. All his life he's been the same: attracting people, then watching them circle around trying to please him like puppy dogs doing tricks. Until they rebel, that is, or he gets bored."

"He's my father," Thorny protested. "I love him. Don't—"

122

"He's my brother," Jenny said, "and I loved him, too. I was almost eighteen before I rebelled. Years and years of wandering around in a fog of constant anxiety. Will John be angry about this? Won't John be pleased I did that? Better not say the other thing. John won't like it. My God, it gives me the shivers just to remember it!"

Thorny stared at her. "*You* were like that, too?"

"Why not?"

"Well, you're too . . . "

"Independent?" Aunt Jenny shrugged. "And so are you, Thorny, love, so are we all, if only we'd realize it. You can't live your life for other people's approval, no matter how much you love them. Because it means they don't really love you if they're not willing to let you be your own person—"

Thorny struggled with tears. "How do you be your own person," she got out at last, "when you don't even know who that person is?"

"You listen to yourself. You stop letting other people tell you what's best. And that includes me," she said, smiling a little.

"Was my . . . my mother like that, too? With Dad, I mean?"

"Her, too," Jenny said. "John was her whole life until you were born, but you can't have a baby and jump at the end of someone else's string, too, not if you love the baby."

Thorny was crying openly now. "Why did she leave me, then?"

"Because he fought her in court for you," Jenny said. "And he had the money to win. Because over the years she'd lost her confidence in herself. Because she wasn't sure any longer she was the best parent for you." She pushed a tissue into Thorny's hand.

"I've never even gone to visit her," Thorny whispered a long time later.

"You will," Jenny said comfortingly. "And now I want you to go to sleep. You've had an exhausting day." Her hand on the light switch, she smiled at her niece. "Patrick and I are very pleased to have you here. Good night, love. Oh, and Thorny—"

"Yes?"

"Try not to have any more dreams that come true, will you? Once is enough for me to gain ten new grey hairs overnight."

To his own disgust Patrick slept like a log. He'd intended to lie awake until he'd thought up some kind of plan to free Alec, but no sooner did he throw himself on the bed than it was morning. He got out of bed. Not yet seven o'clock, and already it was too hot. The sky was empty of birds, a cloudless, burning blue. Smoke was rising from the two back chimneys of Stratton Hall.

The hall clock chimed seven. Fourteen hours until the eclipse. Fourteen hours to disaster. And he and Thorny, the only two people in the world who knew, didn't have the faintest idea how to stop it. If only they could prevent Belman from taking the Keystone out, or at least delay him until after today! After the eclipse the Moon Witch would once again have power to help. If they could make Belman wait until tomorrow, even . . . Briefly Patrick let himself imagine jumping Belman from behind, tying him up and keeping him out of arm's reach until after the eclipse. You and who else, James Bond? he mocked himself. Anyway, even if he could have done it, or by some other means could get Belman out of the way for today, that wouldn't stop him finishing the job another time. And even the Moon Witch couldn't keep the Circle doing its job if there was no Circle there at all!

Patrick slammed his fist into the pillow. If only Alec were free! He'd know what to do! Why else had Belman taken him prisoner? They had to get him out.

He pulled on a pair of jeans and headed for the door. Thorny had slept enough. They simply had to talk. Quietly, so as not to wake his mother, he went down the hall towards Thorny's room. She'd left her door open a crack and he peeked in. But she wasn't in bed. He pushed the door open, unable to believe it. It was true. The sofa-bed had been made up, and Thorny was nowhere to be seen.

17

No Way Out

He was halfway down the drive when he saw her. She was on the main road in front of Stratton Hall, hurrying towards the cottage with her head down, hugging a cardigan-wrapped object close to her body. Patrick stood at the edge of the road and waited for her. His relief was giving way to anger. That was no innocent little stroll she was taking. And what was she carrying?

He stepped out in the roadway to meet her.

"You're out early," she said.

"So are you," he replied pointedly.

"I was going to wake you, but the sun was only just up. Patrick, I had this idea in the middle of the night—"

"You seem to be getting awfully considerate in the middle of the night."

"What do you mean?"

"Well, you didn't wake me the other night, either. And I'm wondering just exactly why."

"I don't have to get your permission every time I leave the house."

"I don't mean that. It's just—"

"What?"

He slouched down, his hands in his pockets. "Nothing," he muttered. "I thought we were in this together."

"I tell you every single thing that happens to me," Thorny protested.

"That's just it," he flared. "It all happens to you. And you make darned sure it does!"

She stared at him. "You're crazy. I can't help it if the Moon Witch's got a thing about me. I can't help it that I can dowse and you can't." With an angry gesture she unwrapped the bundle she was carrying, revealing a willow dowsing stick. "See? I was in Owl Wood, trying something out with this. If you could have helped, I'd have wakened you."

"How do you know I couldn't have helped? Who was it who figured out how important Awen-Un really is? Just because you've decided not to let your fa—people—push you around any more doesn't mean you can do everything without any help."

"It's nothing to do with—" She shook her head and began again. "Look, I had this wild idea, and I wasn't sure if I could do it. I didn't want to try it in front of you until I knew. Not everybody's as sure about things as you are. So do you want to shut up for a change so I can tell you what I've thought of?"

His jaw dropped. Lamely he said, "Well, okay. Sure."

"Oh." A guarded expression settled on her face. "You're going to think it's better than it is."

"Tell me."

"It was something Jeremy said," she told him after a moment. "Do you remember how he said that those old dowsers might have moved the lines of earth-force from one place to another?"

"It was one of his theories," Patrick said cautiously. "But I don't see how anybody could move—" He broke off. "You don't mean to say *you* tried it? And you did it? You actually picked up a line of earth-force and moved it somewhere else?"

"I couldn't do it on my own," she said. "But when I tried it with Alec's medallion—"

"So that's what it's for! No wonder it got hot when you dowsed!" In his excitement he grabbed her arm. "Do you realize what this means? You can do it at Awen-Un, and then it won't matter if Belman finishes off the Circle or not, because all the earth-forces will be somewhere else!"

She took her arm away and covered up the dowsing stick. "I told you you'd think it was better than it was."

"What's the matter? Don't you think you can do it?"

"It would be hard." It had been the most tiring thing she had ever done to pick up that small line of force in Owl Wood and move it out into the churchyard, depositing it under a tombstone there. How could she do it at Awen-Un, where the lines of power were so much stronger? And even then— "The thing is, I'd need time there by myself to try. And Belman—"

"We'll figure out a way for you to be alone," he promised eagerly. "Gosh, Thorny, you are a lucky beast. Did you just tell the medallion you wanted to move the forces, or what? How does it work?"

"I'm not sure," she said. "The medallion's kind of like . . . oh, I don't know, a portable Keystone, maybe. It keeps the power under control, but only if *you're* controlling *it*. You have to dowse the main branch of the current first, and then think your way into it—" She couldn't explain. It was something between the medallion and her, a melding of her mind and its power, working together. But there was something else going on too, something insidious working against what she and the medallion both wanted, something that had its own plans. That, more than anything, worried her.

Patrick's thoughts were racing. "Let's go try it at the Circle right away." He reached for her arm, but she hung back.

"It's no good," she told him. "That man Red is there. That's why I went to Owl Wood to try moving the lines. I figured there'd be earth-forces there, and I . . . didn't want to go into Lady Copse."

"No problem about Red," Patrick said, tugging at her impatiently. "If he's alone, I'll distract him into chasing me off, and you can—" But she only shook her head. What was wrong with her?

"Patrick, you were with Alec when he dowsed the earth-forces at the Circle. It wasn't just a single current, was it?"

"No. I didn't see his map, but it seemed pretty complicated."

"As if every stone had its own current to look after?"

"Well, yes, of course. But not the Keystone. That was the master stone. All the other stones only looked after one current each, but the whole lot came together afterwards in one main branch like the trunk of a tree, and that one went under the Keystone. I'm sure you could move the whole tree if you moved that one branch."

"And where," Thorny asked quietly, "would I move it to?"

Patrick stared at her.

She nodded. "I know. I was pretty excited, too, until I thought of that."

"There's a good-sized standing stone a mile or two from here," Patrick said, thinking frantically. "Over in White-thorn Down. It might do."

"It might do as a Keystone, but what about the other eleven?"

"Do they really matter? As long as all the currents run under the Keystone in the end—"

"But the other eleven stones help control their own parts first. They must be important, Patrick, or they wouldn't have been put there in the first place. And remember, when Belman took away the Keystone the first two times, those eleven did a pretty good job of keeping the forces under control without it."

"But that was because they had the Moon Witch's help," Patrick reminded her. "You said they were crippled until she danced there and made them better."

"I know. But still . . ."

"You're saying we absolutely have to have a Circle with twelve stones?"

"I think we do. I'm sure we do." No way out. *No way but mine.*

He groaned. "Then we're done. The only other stone circle anywhere near here is way over the other side of Swindon, down near Coate Water. And anyway, that one hasn't got twelve stones. Even if it did, how would you get to it? Climb on a bus, with your dowsing stick and Alec's medallion and the earth-forces in tow?''

They were silent then, sunk in gloom. ''It all comes back to Alec,'' Patrick said, pacing up and down. ''It was his medallion. He must have known what it was for. Maybe that's why he came here in the first place, to move the earth-forces away before Belman could destroy the Circle. And if so, he must have had some idea where he was going to move them to. Thorny, we're going to have to get him out.''

''How? We've talked about it and talked about it—''

''If one of us could get into the Hall and hide until the coast was clear—''

''They keep it locked, you said. Windows and doors.''

''You're so negative,'' he accused her. ''Don't you want to get Alec out?''

''Of course I do,'' Thorny protested angrily. ''I'd give anything to see him take care of this whole mess!''

They were quiet then for some time, cudgelling their brains. At last, uncertainly, Thorny said, ''Patrick, if one of us could get *invited* into the Hall, and managed to unlock a door so that the other could sneak in . . . ''

''Yeah, sure. Belman invites the neighbours in to tea every day,'' Patrick said sarcastically.

''Not to tea,'' Thorny said. ''But to see his roses, maybe? He's already asked me. If I took him up on it—''

Patrick stared at her. ''You're crazy,'' he said flatly. ''To begin with, both the greenhouse and the flower garden are outside, not in the house. Second—''

''Maybe he'll give me something to drink,'' she said rapidly. ''It's so hot out. If he didn't I could ask for a glass of water. That would get me inside.''

''What if he caught you unlocking the door?''

''I could pretend I'd tripped over something and unlocked it by accident.''

''And even if he doesn't actually catch you doing it, someone's bound to notice it's unlocked and lock it again before we can use it.''

"Okay, then, suppose I ask for a drink first, before he shows me the roses. Then as soon as you see us in the garden, you'll know I've unlocked the door, and . . . no, that won't work, either. How would you get up to the house without him seeing you?"

"That's not a problem," he said shortly, thinking of his tunnel through the hedge. "You could distract him for a moment, and that'd be all I'd need. But Thorny . . . " He stopped, unable to marshal any more arguments. Why was he so reluctant? It wasn't a bad plan. It gave them a chance, which was more than anything else did. But still . . . *Keep her away from Belman*, Alec had said. And now here they were, planning the exact opposite.

"And you know your way around the Hall, don't you?" Thorny said rapidly. Could she actually want to see Belman again? "You'd know exactly where to hide, and the best places to look for Alec—"

"Okay," he said abruptly.

"We're going to do it?"

"I said, okay," he said irritably.

"What's eating you?"

He scowled at her. "I suppose you realize, if you go up to his door and ask to see his roses, he's going to think you're gooey over him."

"Then that'll make two of you," Thorny said grimly, "won't it?"

Shielded from the road by the stone figures of Virgo and Libra and from the Hall by the hedge, Patrick crouched inside the zodiac and for the last time checked his pockets. Penlight with new batteries, in case Alec was in the cellar. Pocket-knife. Sling-shot. He wasn't going to get caught if he could help it.

It was just after nine o'clock and already he was sweating. Thorny would be knocking on the door to the Hall in just a few minutes. Patrick hoped Belman was still there. They couldn't have made it any earlier, not and have it seem a real social call, but when he'd passed the Hall Patrick had seen Belman loading the landrover with an enormous water breaker, and a basket full of what looked like sticks. He thought about this, squirming through the tunnel. Yesterday Belman had been panting to get at the Keystone again, but the police cordon had prevented him. Today the police were gone, and Belman was fooling around with water and sticks. What was going on?

He was almost through the hedge now, but he stopped where the tangles of yew and briar gave him some cover. A short distance away, with a thick patch of weed-choked gooseberries and a bit of lawn in between, was the back corner of Stratton Hall. Farther on, towards the road, was the door he'd told Thorny to unlock, the one that led into the dining room. That would be the one she'd be likeliest to have a chance at, while someone went into the kitchen to get her a drink. If anyone did. He fixed his eyes on the distant rose-beds and waited.

Nine-thirty, and no Thorny. All this time to get a drink of water? The minutes crawled by. Somewhere not too far away he heard voices, and then the landrover started up. Belman's Swindon lot, Patrick guessed, heading out to the Keystone again. He looked at his watch. Almost ten o'clock, and still no sign of Thorny. Something must have gone wrong.

Grimly he began backing out of the hedge. A loud voice stopped him. Around the corner of the house came the burly Red, head raised to an upstairs window.

"Sife an' sound," he called to whomever was up there. Greaser, probably. Keeping guard on Alec? "Put yer feet up, Alf," Red went on. "'E'll be a couple 'ahrs, anyway . . ."

The inside voice muttered something, and Red nodded. "Yers. Kid went wiv 'im. Crizy over 'im, you can tell. Would've followed 'im right into the 'ahse, if I 'adn't 'a stopped 'er. An' 'im! You'd 'a larfed ter watch 'is nibs workin' on 'er, Alf. Smiled the pants off 'er, near 'nough. Wot's that?"

He laughed crudely. "Yers, 'e likes 'em young, orl right. Kissed 'er 'and, 'e did, an' would 'a done a lot more, if that aunt of 'ers 'adn't come aht an' broke it up. Nahw that one's more my speed, Alf, rahnd an' ready, as they say!"

Patrick did a slow burn. But Red was going on. "Well, I'm orf. Got ter get my beauty sleep. Up since five, guardin' that bloody stone. Give me people, any day. The boss wanted ter know, everyfing locked up orl right? You-know-'oo means a lot ter 'im."

You-know-who. So Thorny was right. Alec was alive, and hidden somewhere in the Hall. And fat lot of good it did to know that, Patrick told himself, backing out of the hedge. In a foul mood, he went to look for her.

She was pacing up and down in Jenny's front garden. When she saw him coming she let out a whoop of relief. "Thank goodness! Boy, was I scared. I thought maybe you'd tried the door and gotten caught." She made a face. "I never even got inside. That Red was like a watch-dog!"

"I know," he said sourly. "He told Greaser, and I heard."

"I had to drink water from the garden hose. And Belman said he'd show me his roses, but not today. He spent most of the time talking to the workmen. Oh, Patrick, it's awful. They're not going to just move the Keystone this time. They're going to break it up!"

"They can't," he said. "It's sarsen stone, one of the hardest rocks there is. It would take them days and days."

"But Belman's got it all figured out. They're going to pour oil on it, then set the oil on fire to make the stone really hot. Then they're going to throw cold water on it. That'll make it crack. They'll hammer wedges into the cracks and soak them to make the wood swell, and that'll break the stone apart. Belman's told them to have the Keystone in pieces by sunset tonight."

Which explained the water breaker and those sticks he'd seen, Patrick thought dazedly. It was the sort of plan Belman wouldn't make mistakes about, either. By tonight there would be no Keystone left. The eclipse was coming, and the Moon

Witch couldn't help, not while the moon was eclipsed. The eleven stones that had been barely able to control the earth-forces with her help would be on their own. Alec in the Hall, but no way to rescue him. Thorny knowing how to use the medallion, but now, with all those men working on the Circle, not able to get near enough to use it—and nowhere to take the forces to, anyway.

Nothing to do. No way out. The sun beat down, savagely triumphant. Patrick turned aside, and without another word went into the house.

18

The Great Heat

The day dragged by. Each hour was hotter than the one before it. By two in the afternoon it was more than a hundred degrees. No one in Wychwood Mount could remember a June afternoon like it. There were no clouds and no wind; only the blazing, breathless sun and the wringing humidity. By three o'clock the bakery, the garage and Jefferson's Grocery had locked their doors, and the White Horse was doing a thriving business. In the post office Aggie Millson sweltered and grumbled, prevented by government regulations from closing early like everyone else. Doctor Wilder's surgery was full of grey-faced people. Jenny Newport was one. She came home and went to bed in the middle of the day, something that ordinarily would have shocked Patrick. But not today. Today nothing surprised him.

In the Circle of Awen-Un Belman strode around the shadeless stones, supervising the burning oil, the great billows of steam, the thudding of the sledgehammer. From the shadows of Lady Copse Thorny and Patrick watched him. Even from here they could see his eyes snapping, alight with the fires that burned on the stone.

"I don't care what anybody says, he's not normal," Patrick declared, but Thorny didn't answer. *Mine enemy, in human guise*, the Lady had said. And sliding into her thoughts, soft as moonlight: *He will not be on guard against thee*. Well, why should he be? She was nothing to him. She was nothing to anybody.

By mid-afternoon the Keystone was in four pieces. The three smaller ones, each weighing several hundred pounds, had been split off from the top of the stone and carted off in the rover. The only piece left was blackened and smoking, less than half its original size. The men had sweated over it for hours. Several cracks were now visible even from Lady Copse. Dozens of wedges had been driven into them. The sounds of splitting stone came like gunshots. And then the ground quivered noticeably. Thorny clutched the medallion under her shirt. The men in the Circle stopped cheering, looking at one another with questioning eyes.

"Going like clockwork," Belman said. "A bonus if the stone's gone before sundown."

But it was hot, it was so hot. They were strong men, and they wanted that bonus, but as time passed they began to falter. One of them fainted. Another, dizzy with heat, got in the way of an oil splash and was badly burned. By four-thirty there were only six men left, and they were muttering amongst themselves. At five o'clock, when a shroud of heat netted the air and the slightest movement was like breathing cotton wool, the leader of the six put down his tools. One after another the rest of the men followed, all except one, who had been toadying up to Belman all afternoon and wasn't going to give up his bonus now. Thorny and Patrick couldn't hear what Belman said, but whatever it was, it made no difference. The five men marched off, leaving Belman staring after them. His face when he turned was like a mask. He snapped an order at the single man who remained, then strode over to the landrover and drove off.

"Anybody normal would be calling it quits for today," Patrick said.

"Well, maybe he *is* quitting," Thorny said. "Maybe he *is* normal. Maybe . . . "

"Sure. That's why he just about stood on his head to get those men to finish the job by sunset. He doesn't care that the eclipse is coming, and that the Moon Witch will be at her weakest then. He doesn't know Awen-Un's her Master

Circle, and that destroying it will just about destroy her. He doesn't even know there is such a thing as a Moon Witch. Oh, no, he's just nice ordinary Squire Belman, and he's going home to supper and his comfy little bed . . . '' His voice was cutting.

Thorny didn't answer. Patrick saw her hand close on the medallion hidden under her shirt. Then she ran off. And on her face, for the first time, Patrick saw decision.

"Twelve things," she said, "all in a circle. What does that make you think of?"

Dinner was over. It had been a short, silent meal, with Jenny in bed and neither Thorny nor Patrick able to eat much. "Awen-Un," Patrick said dourly. "A clock . . . Thorny, we've got to get Alec out, we've simply got to!"

"We tried. It didn't work. Anyway—"

"Belman will be back over at the Circle by now. And he'll be needing Red, for sure, to help that other man get the rest of the Keystone out. That just leaves Greaser to guard Alec. Two of us against his one. I'm sure we could do it."

"No," Thorny said.

He stared at her. "What?"

"Patrick, listen. It's too late to get Alec out. No, listen. Even if we could do it, and he could get the medallion over to the Circle, wouldn't Belman be watching Alec pick up those forces and move them somewhere else? Then wouldn't Belman just go there and do exactly what he's doing to Awen-Un?"

"How do I know? There isn't anything else to try. Maybe we could distract Belman. Give Alec a chance to do his thing without anybody seeing—"

"You said Belman was sure Awen-Un was the Master Circle. Okay, if he's that sure, suppose he destroys Awen-Un and nothing horrible happens?"

"He'll think he was wrong," Patrick said defiantly. "He'll think Awen-Un was just ordinary after all."

"With Alec on the loose? Come on, Patrick. He's going to know Alec's moved those forces! And with only a few minutes to do it in, don't you think Belman would figure out that Alec moved the forces someplace nearby?"

"But there isn't anywhere nearby! It has to be twelve stones in a circle, you said it yourself. There isn't anything like that near here!"

"What about the zodiac?"

The breath whooshed out of him. Statues of stone, all in a circle. "Yes, there are twelve! And they're made of sarsen, too, the same as Awen-Un. Thorny, you're a genius!"

"Somebody still has to move the forces there," she reminded him, not at all joyfully. *Avoid me how thou will* . . .

"You said you could do it, if there was someplace to move them to. And now there is, and it's right here in Wychwood Mount!" Excitedly, Patrick slapped his fist into his palm. "And afterward, when Belman finishes off the Circle and nothing happens, he'll just have to think he was wrong about Awen-Un being the Master Circle. I mean, with Alec a prisoner, and nobody else to move the forces—"

"He does know the medallion's missing. If he knows what it's for—"

"He thinks Alec's hidden it, that's all." Thorny frowned doubtfully. "You don't seem very pleased," he said. "What's wrong? Don't you think you can do it?"

"It's just not . . . simple. For one thing, I'll have to be able to dowse there, to find that main branch of the earth-forces you told me about, the one you said was like the trunk of a tree. That'll take time, and Belman's there. How am I going to keep him from seeing me?"

"We'll distract him."

"Long enough for me to sneak in and do it?"

"We'll wait till it's dark."

"That's when the eclipse is going to start," she reminded him. "It doesn't leave a lot of time. And what if he uses a light? No, I've got to get into the Circle openly and make him trust me. Then maybe I'll have a chance to—"

"So what're you going to do, enlist in his little stone-breaking party?" Silence. He stared at her, outraged. "You don't mean it?"

"Why not? I could make up to him a little . . . tell him I'd like to watch, something like that. He won't say no, not if he really is working against the Moon Witch—"

"If!"

"—and if he's guessed she wanted me to help her, what with my name being Hawthorn and all. He'd be happy to have me on his side, just to spite her. Then later, when it got dark enough, and he was sure enough of me, I might get a chance to do the dowsing, and—"

"Might."

"It's the best I can think of, Patrick!"

For a long moment he was silent. Then he said, "I don't like it one bit."

Thorny threw her head back. "I knew you wouldn't! You've got some kind of crazy idea that I *like* Belman. What do I have to do to prove—?"

"All right, all right," Patrick said wearily. "But I still don't like the idea of you going in there tonight and sucking up to him."

"I didn't say I was going to suck up to him," she said stiffly. "I said I was going to *act* as if I—"

"I know what you said. Look, you say you don't like Belman, and that's fine by me. But if it's true, and you do go in there, you're going to have to do the best acting job in the world to convince him you're on his side, or he'll be so suspicious of you he'll watch you even harder." He chewed his lip while she stared at him stonily. "Okay," he got out at last, "so you're going over to join him. Why don't I pretend to want to stop you, and yell and hop around a bit when you start your act with him? If he thinks I'm mad at you, he might be more ready to believe you really are on his side."

"I don't know," she said. "You . . . well, you're not much of an actor, Patrick. Belman might guess you were only pretending. But I suppose if you just sort of grabbed me, and didn't say anything . . . "

"And what am I supposed to do while you're oohing at Belman and dowsing and moving the earth-forces? Sit quietly by and watch?"

"Whatever you do," Thorny said, with a wild little laugh, "I'll bet it won't be that."

19

The Eclipse Begins

Shortly after eight the full moon began to rise. The heat made it shimmer, a silvery circle whose edges were not quite firm. Low in the northwest the sun opposed it, though sunset was well under way. For ten minutes, no more, sun and moon were in the sky at the same time. Then the sun set. Twilight set in, grey and formless.

Billows of steam surrounded the Keystone. Under Belman's supervision Red and the Swindon workman were hard at it again, readying a whole new lot of wedges from the bushel basket. "All they need now is three good splits," Patrick muttered. Thorny knew what he meant. Break what was left of the Keystone into four, and a couple of men could handle the fragments easily. And then there would be no Keystone left, and only she would remain to forestall disaster. She clutched the cardigan-wrapped dowsing stick to her chest, white-faced and trembling, her eyes huge brown pools of uncertainty. Patrick frowned. Some actor she was turning out to be. And she had said *he* was bad!

"You look awful," he told her roughly. "Lighten up, will you?"

Belman had seen them coming over the rise that overlooked Awen-Un. He sent Thorny a long, piercing look. Flushing, she returned it, then dropped her eyes, stumbling so that Patrick had to take her arm. Something about that mute exchange worried Patrick. "Thorny, are you sure you—?"

Thorny spun on her heel so quickly that Patrick was taken by surprise. "Hey!" he said. But she was already halfway down the hill. He had been supposed to grab her. How was he to do that, if she wouldn't let herself get caught? He ran after her. Didn't she think he could handle the big, important role she'd given him? Disobeying her rule, he shouted after her. She paid no attention. Belman was still watching. In the grey dimness his face stood out, a black-and-white portrait, all shadows and glitter and dark, calculating eyes. He was the enemy. Why had Thorny never admitted it? Patrick ran faster.

"Thorny!" he shouted, a kind of panic in his voice. She looked back, slowing slightly. And with a final burst of speed he closed in on her.

He grabbed her free arm more violently than he'd intended, and they both almost fell. "Leave me alone!" Thorny shouted.

"You do like him, don't you?"

"Let go!" And she broke free, darting away from him, heading for the Circle, and Belman.

Patrick stopped, frozen to the footpath, doubt settling in. Acting, that was all it had been. Thorny had been acting, just as she had said she would. In the Circle Belman was greeting her, the planes of his face drawn upwards, the shadows beneath them deepening.

"By all means," Patrick heard, through the *thwack-thwack-thwack* of the sledgehammers. "I rather thought you might show up." Shame tore at Patrick, shame for Thorny, that she could smile at Belman like that. And Belman took Thorny's arm and led her around, showing her this and pointing to that, while in the growing gloom Patrick watched, dark and doubting. And all the time the sledgehammers kept up their gut-wrenching destruction, and the Keystone steamed.

Defiantly Patrick sat down cross-legged, facing Awen-Un. But no one appeared to notice. In the Circle the men stopped hammering. In the silence that remained, Patrick thought he heard something. Pale and high and shrill, like a scream or a hiss . . . . He quivered, or the ground did, and he put both hands down on it, outstretched. Then he looked up. The eclipse was beginning.

A second ago the moon had been a circle. Now a tiny bite had been taken out of its left side. Patrick jumped to his feet. His legs felt wobbly, as if they didn't really belong to him. In the Circle someone was screaming: the Swindon man, Patrick saw through eyelashes gummed together in a sudden blur of static. The labourer's hair was crackling; everyone's was. A whirligig of dried grasses and leaves surrounded the man, drawn like magnets to the charge he bore. He man-handled them away, screaming and shaking his hands as if they were on fire. He had been touching the Keystone, which now glowed a pale, silvery blue. Somewhere there was a hum like high-tension wires, the crackle of fire taking hold. With a sound like tearing cloth the ground opened. One of Awen-Un's smaller stones teetered like a tenpin and fell. Another. God! Thorny was on the ground, dragging herself towards the Keystone, towards Belman. And Belman, who had never before seemed so inhuman, reached calmly for the pail of water by his feet, and threw it on the Keystone.

Crackle! Hiss! Blue light flamed out from the Keystone like a Roman candle. Then blue changed to white, a single blinding flare. For a moment the stone seemed to grow, a mountain. Then, spent, it faded. The world steadied, grew quiet. Near the centre of the Circle the Swindon man sat licking his hands like an animal. Minute followed minute, and nothing else happened. In the deepening gloom the Key-stone was small and lifeless. Was it over, then? Patrick asked himself. Was that all there was to the Moon Witch's threats? The moon was darkening, and the earth remained. Why did he feel that he ought to be holding his breath?

"Enough," Belman said, sudden and peremptory. "You both have work to do." And he nodded towards the Keystone. "Red, the oil. And you—" He jerked his head at the Swindon man "—you carry on with what you were doing."

The wounded man staggered to his feet. "My hands," he blubbered. "How d'you expect me to work with these?" And

143

he held them out, all blistered and raw. Belman took a step towards him, but the man backed away. "Don't touch me! That hellstone's yours, innit? Plain as a pikestaff there's not much to pick and choose between the pair o' you."

"If you're not going to work," Belman said coolly, "you can leave."

"What about my bonus?"

"You were promised a bonus when the Keystone was gone. It's not gone."

"But—"

With a bored gesture Belman turned away, looking up at the sky to where the moon was slowly being eaten by darkness. For a long moment he stared at it thoughtfully. Then he laughed. No one knew what he was laughing at. Behind him the workman yammered something, then, wringing his hands, left. Red picked up the sledgehammer. Like rat-scrabblings in a condemned building, the hiss and hum of electricity was beginning again. And above their heads the moon darkened.

In the shadows Thorny was as motionless as a thirteenth stone. The hum like power-lines was audible to everyone, but with only a single glance at Belman Red refilled the bucket of water and hastily poured the water on the wedges. The stone hissed like a snake, but nothing else happened. Patrick groaned to himself. Do it, Thorny. Get that dowsing *done!* But she crouched, silent and still, while the wedges swelled and strained against the Keystone and the world darkened.

C-R-A-C-K! It was like a rifle shot. Belman gave a nod. "That's a clean break," he said to Red, his voice carrying clearly.

Red went over to the Keystone. A kerosene lamp flickered to life. "Split right open, it 'as, top to bottom," Red announced, holding the lamp high over the stone. "Practikly the 'ole front 'alf we got 'ere."

"Get it into the rover, then," Belman said.

Red frowned doubtfully, but bent over the newly fragmented piece of Keystone. His enormous arms strained like

144

knotted ropes, but he managed to slide only the front edge of the fragment up and out of its hole. "'Eavy little devil," he grunted, "Goin' ter be 'ard for me ter do it alone."

Belman threw his head back. "Try it again," he ordered.

Groaning with exertion Red leaned over the rock once more. Thorny got to her feet and came a little closer, then bent and picked up the lamp. "'Ere now, wotcher doin' wiv that flasher?" Red panted angrily.

"I'll hold it for you," she said. "Then you can see better."

"Hurry up," Belman said with a glance at the moon. It was almost a quarter eaten away, and getting darker by the minute.

"I dunno if I can, not alone," Red said. "Must weigh three, four 'unnert pounds."

Belman shook his head. "I'll have to help you, I suppose." He pulled a pair of gloves from his pocket, then took off his jacket, laying it on one of the stones. It was so quiet that Patrick could hear the keys jangling in the jacket pocket. Frowning a little, Belman put the gloves on. So he didn't want to touch the stone, either. More than anything else so far, that made Patrick afraid.

A minute passed. Belman and Red were heaving on the stone. Thorny had gone around behind it, stepping into the hole the fragment had left, holding the lantern high. Helpful of her, Patrick thought bitterly. She had left the dowsing stick behind, wrapped in her cardigan on the edge of the hole. Why wasn't she using this time to do her dowsing, while Belman was occupied with the Keystone? Why was she in the stone-hole at all? But now the two men were on their feet again, staggering under the weight of the rock fragment.

They backed away from the hole it had left, then man-oeuvred it around so they could head for the rover. Patrick willed Thorny to action. Belman had his back to her, and Red was too busy trying to walk backwards and carry the stone to watch Thorny. Go on, Thorny, get your dowsing stick. Do it before they get to the rover! For a minute he thought she would. She got as far as putting the lantern down. Then a lot of things happened at once.

From the Keystone there came another loud crack of splitting stone. Belman, who was in the rear, turned his head sharply. In that moment of inattention the stone in the men's hands shifted, so that for a few seconds the entire weight of the rock-fragment was being supported by Red. Any normal man would have dropped it, but Red was too strong for his own good. Somehow he hugged it to his chest just long enough to stagger back against the open back of the land rover. There, the terrible weight of the stone upended him. He screamed, once. Then his arms gave way, and the stone rolled down his chest and onto his face. There was a horribly wet, crushing sound. A ghastly silence fell.

For a moment everyone seemed frozen. Belman moved then, going over to the rear of the rover from which Red's motionless legs still protruded. His hand reached in. After a few seconds he turned his head towards Thorny. In the lamp-light she was as white as new snow.

"Is he—" she began.

"Dead," Belman nodded. "A pity. He was a strong man. And there's still a good six hundred pounds of Keystone to be moved."

He looked at Thorny. He'd forgotten Patrick. Wide-eyed with loathing, Patrick stared at him. His own servant was dead, and that was all he could say! He tore his eyes away to see what Thorny would do. Her face was working. Surely now she would see that Belman was something to be fought to the end!

"I'm not as strong as . . . Red," she said. "But I . . . I'll help you."

Patrick stood numb with shock, trying to disbelieve his ears. To help Belman . . . to destroy the Keystone . . . she couldn't! She was still pretending to be under his influence— that was it! Now that Belman had no one else to distract him

146

she had to play for time, make him trust her until she had a chance to . . .

Briefly Patrick closed his eyes, praying that she didn't mean it, that at the last minute she would turn the tables on Belman and defeat him. And when he opened his eyes again the Moon Witch was there.

20

Betrayal

Patrick knew it was the Moon Witch. She was Thorny's age, and his mother's age, and Eve's; she was the most beautiful woman in the world and the ugliest. She wore a long white gown and a robe that was in tatters and she had eyes that made Patrick shudder.

"Usurper," she addressed Belman. "Thinkest thou to turn Hawthorn to thine own ends?"

"She chose me freely, Witch," Belman smiled. "She is her own person."

Thorny was huddled into the space beside the Keystone. She kept looking from one of them to the other, but neither noticed. They were arguing about her, but they didn't even bother to look at her.

"She will not obey thee," the Lady said. "Whatever she says, she is no puppet of thine."

Belman took a step nearer. "And if not my puppet, whose? How many years have you planned this, risking all on this girl? Look at her! Does she seem to be yours? Do her eyes light up when she looks at you?"

The Lady shimmered, white as moonlight, and as cold. "Hawthorn knows the shame of that kind of worship. Be not proud, Puppet Master. What she feels for thee is only an accident of likenesses."

"Accident?" Belman sneered. "And who of hers am I like, so accidentally?" Then, his voice cold with understanding, "Ah, yes. Her father. Yes, I see. Is there nothing you will not do, Witch, to get rid of me?"

The Lady smiled. "Thy defeat, when it comes, will be utter."

"Defeat! Do you think I can be defeated now? When Awen-Un is gone there will be nothing left for you on this world. A stone away," Belman's voice rang out. "That is all I am, a stone away from your defeat!"

"Then let it be thy gravestone!"

Belman didn't move. "I am in human form," he reminded her, calm and sure. "You cannot harm me. Only another human—"

The Moon Witch raised her arm. "And what is Hawthorn?"

Belman smiled. "And how shall she harm me? Am I to be kissed to death? Or—" He broke off. Thorny had bent and straightened so quickly that only Patrick had seen the movement. And in her hand, now pointing with a desperate kind of steadiness at Belman, was the gun that had disappeared the night the Keystone had returned.

Patrick felt as if he were suffocating. So that was what had happened to it! Thorny must have dug it into the Keystone's socket, and then the stone had returned, hiding it from the police. And now she had it again, and was aiming it at Belman.

"I have to kill you," she said. Her voice was toneless as fate.

"Foolish child," Belman said, but softly, gently. "Why?"

"You're going to destroy the world."

"That isn't why."

"I . . . she . . . "

"She wants you to, Thorny. That is why. You have to kill me because she wants you to. Everyone has always wanted something from you. Aren't you tired of it? Aren't you tired of being used? She will make you a murderer. You, a human

149

being with a mind and heart of your own, are to be her weapon. You are a tool, Thorny, *her* tool.''

The Lady spoke, calm, cold, sure as death. ''Remember Awen-Un, Hawthorn. He will tear it down, and there will be nothing left. Death, destruction, chaos, despair. Wilt thou let it happen? Only thou canst stop it. Only thou! He is what thy father is, Hawthorn. He is a Puppet Master, controlling with strings of soft words, of gestures, of charm. He wants worship, not love. And in return he gives nothing! He will take from thee, and take and take, and when thou art dry of giving he will cast thee aside, and thou wilt have nothing left, not even thine own self.''

''And she will not take from you? She will not cast you aside when you have done what she asks and the courts and jails and asylums of this world await? She deceives everybody,'' Belman said. ''She uses everything.''

The gun wavered. Thorny blinked desperately.

''I love thee. I will not abandon thee.''

''She is your mother, Thorny! She is all our mothers! And in the end she abandons us all.''

With a cry of despair and fury Thorny swung the gun away from Belman and towards the Moon Witch. ''It was you, you all along!'' she raged. ''My whole life . . . my father, my mother . . . oh, God, what else? All along, every step of the way, wrecking my life, using me! And lying to me, lying. You didn't care about Awen-Un, you didn't care about me—'' And her hand clenched, the finger on the trigger tightening.

Patrick was running forward. ''Don't do it, Thorny!'' he shouted. ''Belman's using you against her. It's the Circle that ma—''

It was too late. Five shots exploded again and again, making more noise than a dozen splitting Keystones. The Moon

150

Witch shattered, glassy shards carrying a thousand images of her fury and despair into the darkness.

Patrick ran on. Thorny had made her choice. She'd betrayed them all, made herself Belman's thing. And that meant that there was only one thing left to do. It was probably too late, but he had to try it. Grabbing Belman's jacket from the stone where he'd laid it, Patrick ran on, fumbling in the pockets for the keys to the Hall, hearing neither Belman's triumphant laughter nor the hopeless sound of Thorny's sobs.

Alec was his only hope. He had to rescue Alec.

He went overland, across the ancient moors that were now Belman's. It was a rough route, but fast, and one the jeep could not follow. When he reached the main road he slipped across and climbed the hedge.

The eclipse was far advanced now, the moon already less than half its proper size. He kept looking at it, even though he knew it didn't matter anymore. Before, they'd known that until the moon went completely dark they could rely on at least some help from the Moon Witch to hold the Circle to its job, even if Belman finished off the Keystone first. Now there was no Moon Witch, and it all relied on the Keystone. Once it was gone, the earth-forces would erupt like a volcano. Patrick had to get Alec over to the Circle before that, and somehow get him his medallion back so he could move the forces. Alec would figure out how. But first Patrick had to free him.

The front door to the Hall was brightly lit, but it was also the quickest, and right now speed mattered more than anything. Patrick had taken about fifteen minutes to reach the Hall. Even with only Thorny to help, Belman must have had time to get at least one more piece of Keystone into the rover. Would they move Red's body first, Patrick wondered a little light-headedly, or would they just pile the stones on top of him?

He made for the front door and fumbled through Belman's keys. On the fifth try he got it. Nervously, he pushed the door open.

No one was in the foyer. The grand staircase was dimly lit and silent, the upstairs landing dark. Down the hall to the left and right everything was black. But straight ahead in the kitchen a light was on and a radio was playing. This decided Patrick. Until now he hadn't been certain whether to try the cellar first or the attic. But as the cellar steps went down from the kitchen, he clearly ought to try the attic first. He tiptoed up the staircase, hugging the railing and keeping low. Halfway up he peered over the railing into the kitchen. Greaser was there. He was sitting at a chrome-legged table playing solitaire, a row of empty bottles at his elbow. *Slap-slap-slap*, went the cards on the table. Then he cursed, long and creatively, and began to gather the cards in for another attempt. Patrick ducked, half crawling the rest of the way up.

Patrick knew the attic well, having spent rainy summer days there since he was six. At the door, he went through Belman's keys. An old-fashioned one, he thought feverishly, for an old-fashioned lock. There! That one! He tried it. The door opened easily. Quickly Patrick flashed his penlight around. It didn't take him long to find what he was looking for. There on a wooden bench against the wall, gagged, trussed like a chicken, but with eyes as angry and defiant as a chained hawk, was Alec.

"Where's Thorny?"

They were Alec's first words, and he got them out even before Patrick had cut his gag completely away. Silently Patrick cut through the rope around Alec's wrists. Then he

152

started on the one at his feet. "She's in the Circle," he managed at last, "helping Belman."

Alec was bending over, massaging his feet. At Patrick's words he went very still. Slowly he raised his head. "And the medallion?" he said, his voice remote. "Did she give it to him?"

"Not yet. She will, though. She's done everything else for him, including killing the white lady."

"Killing the—?"

"You know. The Moon Witch. Thorny's shot her, and she's dead. The Keystone's almost gone, and Belman and Thorny are—"

"The eclipse?" Alec demanded, staggering a little as he got to his feet. "How long till total darkness?"

"Twenty minutes, maybe, half an hour. I don't know. Anyway, the moon doesn't matter now that the Moon Witch is dead."

Alec was stamping his feet quietly, trying to get the numbness out. "Any guards here?"

"One," Patrick said, "in the kitchen."

"Red?"

"No, Greaser. Red's dead. Part of the Keystone—"

"Let's get out of here first," Alec said. "You can tell me everything else on the way."

They crept down the stairs, peering into the kitchen as they went by. Greaser had his head on his arms and was snoring. One of the empty bottles had fallen to the floor and was smashed. Alec smiled coldly. "A pretty scene," he said softly. "One Belman won't easily forgive." They locked the front door behind them, then made for the footpath as fast as Alec's rubbery legs could go.

"How long were you in there?" Patrick asked him, when Alec began to move easily enough to have attention to spare.

"Too long." They'd taken him prisoner on Wednesday night, he told Patrick. "There was no trace of Belman in the business world, no record of his birth at Somerset House, nothing. I wanted to talk to him about it. Well, it turned out he wanted to talk to me even more." He grimaced. "Now tell me what's been happening to you. The whole lot, please. Start after I left on Wednesday."

With only a few short, sharp questions he let Patrick speak uninterrupted. High in the sky rode the crippled moon, the blackness devouring it little by little. There was only a crescent left now, a sliver. "Blast these legs!" Alec said once, looking up, and tried to hurry faster. Patrick was worried, too. Belman and Thorny might easily have finished breaking up the Keystone by now. No, he corrected himself, they couldn't have finished. If they had, the world would have known it.

Patrick trotted on, tugging at Alec's sleeve, trying by the force of his will to make him go faster. Then they were slogging their last few steps up the hill that overlooked the Circle. Patrick's heart was hammering when at last they were at the top. He wanted to rush on at once, but Alec grabbed his arm from behind.

And then together they looked down upon the Circle.

21

The End of the Keystone

In the night that had finally come, Patrick and Alec could see little of Awen-Un—only the small area near the Keystone illuminated by the lantern. Within that pale circle were Belman and Thorny, straining together on what was left of the Keystone: a piece of rock no bigger than a pumpkin. So small! Patrick's heart thumped. It wouldn't take them more than a few minutes to get that out of the ground.

He turned a frantic face to Alec. "Let's go! Now!"

"Not quite yet." Alec was very grave, but calm. His hold on Patrick's arm tightened. "Listen to me. Here's what you have to do. Run for the lantern and break it. Whatever happens to me, get rid of that light, do you hear?"

"What about Thorny? Do you want me to try and take the medallion from her?"

"No. *No*. And whatever you do, say *nothing* about it."

"Then how are you going to move the—"

"Let me worry about that." Above their heads the moon flickered. It was a line, pencil-thin, the darkness around it vast and threatening. Sounds were everywhere: whistles, creaks, groans, sighs. Sounds on the edge of awareness, creeping to consciousness. Patrick thought of an enormous body in a cage awakening after a long sleep. The moon went fainter still, dying; and suddenly darkness devoured her.

Patrick felt Alec's hand drop from his arm and shove him forward.

He was running, Alec behind him, into the Circle. No moon, no light, only the lantern. A tiny piece of Keystone on one side, and the whole vast earth on the other, shaking its cage, breaking free. And Thorny there in the centre, bending over the Keystone, prying at it, killing it as she had killed the Moon Witch. *How could she?* Rage filled Patrick, and hatred. Hatred for those long, white fingers that scrabbled for destruction, hatred for that tear-smeared face and dripping forehead, hatred for those eyes of hers that sought Belman out.

From the darkness he shouted at her, the worst words he could think of, terrible words brimming with hatred, spilling like acid. He pounded into the Circle, his hands reaching for her. He wanted to feel those white fingers breaking under his feet. He wanted to smash her face against the stone. He wanted to hurt her as much as she had hurt him.

Belman saw him coming and stepped to one side, waiting for Alec. Thorny scrambled backwards, the despair on her face sending a fierce joy through Patrick. Something was in his path. He kicked at it, hardly noticing. The lantern went over, flickered half-heartedly and died. Darkness fell.

Pitch-black. Belman, shining, a bronze in black velvet. Thorny. Where was she? He could hear her crying. He shouted again, something obscene about the uses of crocodile tears. Someone laughed. The ground shivered, pitching and tossing, stones rattling, falling. Patrick flailed in the darkness but encountered nothing. He fell. For a moment he lay still, his mouth sour and dry, tainted by the words that had poured out of it. He'd never known such violence, never realized what it was that lurked inside him, waiting.

Thorny was gone, he knew it. Tired to the bone, he dragged himself to his feet and turned around. It was then that he saw Belman. He seemed to produce his own light, a spectral green emanation that was bright enough to illuminate someone else: Alec, on the ground in front of him.

It took a moment for Patrick to realize what was going on. In that moment Belman kicked Alec, and as he writhed, followed it up with another kick to the neck. Somehow Alec twisted out of the way in time. But he was getting the worst of it, that was clear. Patrick began to run towards them. Alec was upright again, though teetering. He shot out a fist. It didn't connect. Belman had the balance of a cat. He alone seemed not to feel the unsteadiness of the ground. He danced out of Alec's reach and in again. Steadily, almost caressingly, he reached for Alec's throat.

"If you kill me," Alec gasped out, staggering, "you can't remain in human form. And then *she*—"

Belman smiled at the moonless sky, and his gloved fingers choked off Alec's voice. "She doesn't matter now," he said. "Make your farewells, Old One."

Putting on a final burst of speed, Patrick tackled Belman from the side. It was a good tackle, but it didn't bring Belman down. All it did was make Patrick recoil as if he'd come into contact with molten steel. He fell to the ground, burning. He tried to get up again and couldn't. Alec's eyes were protruding. His hands had stopped flailing. Grimly Patrick summoned all his strength. With a last desperate effort he reached into his pocket. His hands found his pocket-knife, opened it, and threw.

The knife glanced against Belman's leg, not enough to do any real damage, but distracting. His hands relaxed their hold, and Alec slid to the ground. Patrick could hear him breathe, hoarse and raspy, alive but unconscious.

Belman rubbed his wounded leg thoughtfully, watching Patrick with the indifference of a judge. The light that surrounded him seemed paler.

"I hope you didn't break that lantern," he said at last, then turned away, peering into the darkness. "Thorny. Thorny!" But there was no reply. "I seem to have lost my helper," Belman said then, an ironic twist to his lips. "I wonder why."

Patrick flushed. He knew why Thorny had run away, and so did Belman. "Fetch the lantern," Belman ordered him.

"Fetch it yourself. I'm not a dog." The world was going to end, and he wasn't going to lick Belman's boots while it did.

Belman looked bored. "I believe you care for this Old One," he said, and dug the toe of his shoe into Alec's neck.

It was a veiled threat, but it worked. No matter how close the end of the world was, Patrick couldn't just lie there and watch Belman kill Alec. He scrambled to his feet, swaying slightly.

"Leave him alone," he said. "I'll get your bloody lantern."

It took him five minutes, while the ground trembled intermittently: normalcy for a time, then a violent quake, then a series of little quivers like an animal shaking itself after a drenching. Belman waited, his restless eyes striving to pierce the dark that surrounded them.

"Hurry," he said as Patrick fumbled with the lantern's door and felt for the wick, trying to find some matches in the mess in his pocket. At last the light shone out. Belman nodded. "Now for the Keystone."

Patrick felt sick. Not the Keystone, too! He remembered how revolted he'd been, seeing Thorny helping Belman with the stone. Now it was his turn: forced into the final betrayal, to destroy the world or watch as Alec died. What kind of choice was that?

"Please don't—" he pleaded, but Belman shook his head.

"You will hold the lantern." He turned away, making for the stone. Patrick took up the lantern and moved in, drawn in passive terror to the small, dirty, broken piece of Keystone that was the world's foundation.

Belman bent over the stone, taking one side in each gloved hand. It was a long moment, endless as a nightmare. Patrick stood frozen. Then, with a wrench, the moment ended. The stone was a victory sign in Belman's hands, no part of it in contact with the earth. Patrick stared at the empty stone-hole, at the other stones scattered and fallen, at the ruin that Awen-Un had become. Slowly he lowered himself to the ground and waited for what was to come.

The lantern trembled, and he took it into his lap to steady it. He watched Belman as if he were a book to be memorized. Belman still held the Keystone aloft, but his victory sign had gone stale. It was too long. He had committed what ought to have been the world's greatest blasphemy, and nothing had happened. The ground trembled, but no more than before, and the terrible groan of an earth awakening had died to silence. And Belman, with a face like a death-mask, lowered his hands and let the Keystone fall on the ground.

"She deceives everyone," he said. "She has always deceived everyone. I should have listened when I told Thorny so."

"She?" Patrick asked, just as if Belman were somebody normal, somebody who would explain. "The Moon Witch, you mean?"

"She wanted me dead," Belman said, "but she had to invent a reason, or Thorny wouldn't kill me." And he turned a savage smile on Patrick and barked out a laugh.

"Invent? You mean . . . she fooled you? Awen-Un wasn't . . . isn't . . . " He broke off, his voice a squeak. Here they were, no Keystone and no Moon Witch, and with all those earth-forces let loose, the world should have been ripping itself to shreds. But it wasn't! Was Belman right? Had the Moon Witch deceived them? Was Awen-Un really not her Master Circle after all?

Feverishly he considered it. There must be some earth-forces at Awen-Un, or there wouldn't have been those fireworks earlier. But not *all* the earth-forces of the whole world. The Moon Witch must have just made Thorny's rod dip that day in Lady Copse, when they'd been sure so many lines of force were there. Combined with her dire predictions and a Keystone that kept coming back on its own, it had seemed to prove how important Awen-Un was to the world, and that the man who was destroying it ought to be destroyed himself. It was a sure-fire plan: the perfect way for the Moon Witch, who couldn't do it herself, to get Belman killed.

Except that Belman hadn't let it happen. He had taken Thorny's anger and pointed it at the Moon Witch instead. And then it had turned out to be a standoff after all. The Moon Witch hadn't gotten Belman killed, but neither had

Belman found her Master Circle. The world wasn't going to end because Awen-Un was destroyed. The world wasn't going to end at all!

Patrick looked up. Then, cheering wildly, he leapt to his feet.

The moon was coming out again.

"It was all for nothing!" he crowed into Belman's mask of a face. "The Moon Witch made it all up, and you fell for it, Belman. She's made a fool out of you!"

Instantly Belman changed. He wasn't a man, he wasn't even alive. Now he was a great sphere of burning bronze—hard, lifeless, pitiless. Now a horned face with serpents for hair and fire in its heart; now an all-encompassing cage of eternal torments; now a desert lost in a merciless sun. Image after image, layers of hell unfolding like an onion; and always deeper, always unassailable, the heart, the true being.

"Who is the fool?" Patrick heard, or thought he heard. "Think on this, Patrick Newport. When the last of the Moon Witch's circles is gone, remember what you have said, and remember me. I will come for you then, wherever you have crawled away to hide, however many years pass before that time. I will come to you, and I will watch you realize who is a fool and who is not!"

And then he was gone. Body first, shimmer next, hot deadly eyes last of all. And then nothing, nothing of him at all, only the memory.

22

Recovery

"Rather foolish of you to taunt him like that." It was Alec's voice coming from behind. "I'm afraid you may be sorry for it some day."

Patrick turned to see Alec sitting up on one elbow, watching him. "I'm sorry for it now," he admitted. But Belman was gone, and the world was not. It was hard not to be cheerful. "How long have you been awake? Did you hear about Awen-Un?"

"Oh, yes, I heard."

"Isn't it marvellous? Awen-Un nothing after all! I can't believe how much we worried about it, and now . . . . . What're you looking like that for?"

Alec shook his head. "For someone rather bright, Patrick, you can be—"

"What are you talking about?"

"I'm talking about you, and what you are willing to believe, and what not."

"What do you mean?"

"Not here," Alec said, getting to his feet. He took Patrick by the arm and without another word led him out of the Circle. When they were safe in the garden of Patrick's cottage, he said, "Do you think I might sleep on your sofa tonight? I'll be away early, and the village will have enough to talk about in the morning without me turning up at the White Horse at this hour, too."

"Sure. Mum won't mind when she hears what's happened."

"Your version?" Alec asked dryly. "Or the truth?"

"Alec, what's going on? You keep hinting and hinting, and I—"

"Didn't you tell me Thorny was going to try to move the earth-forces?"

"Yes, but—"

"And didn't you tell me she was going to pretend to be on Belman's side until she had a chance to do it?"

"She had a chance," Patrick said hostilely, "and she didn't use it."

"You mean, I suppose, those few seconds when Belman and Red were carrying that hunk of Keystone between them? Wasn't that the very moment that she must have discovered the gun again, and remembered what the Moon Witch wanted her to do with it? The shock of that, on top of everything else—"

"Alec, she didn't just pretend to be on Belman's side. She killed the Moon Witch! I told you!"

"Come now, Patrick, use your head. She didn't kill anybody."

"What? Alec, I was there, I saw it! The Moon Witch burst into a million pieces—"

"Her image did, you mean. *She* is as alive as she ever was. She never existed in this world any more than Belman would have, had he not taken human form. How do you shoot a ghost?"

"But . . . Thorny thought she was killing her!"

"Did she really? When she knew the Moon Witch couldn't hurt Belman, nor he her, simply because he was in human form and she was not? If Belman couldn't hurt the Moon Witch, how could Thorny think *she* could?"

Had Thorny really been just pretending? Had it all been just an elaborate ploy so that Belman would be sure she was on his side? No. He wouldn't believe it. "Alec, Thorny *wanted* to hurt her! If you could have just seen her face—"

"And have you never wanted to hurt anybody?" Alec asked softly.

Patrick flushed painfully, remembering how violently he had wanted to do that very thing. Violence. Maybe it was there inside everybody. "But Thorny helped Belman destroy the Keystone!"

"Which you would have done, too, if he had wanted."

"But only to save your life!"

"And maybe," Alec said gently, "Thorny did it to save quite a lot of lives."

Patrick bit down on his lip. Thorny digging at the Keystone waiting for darkness, for her chance to get away without Belman seeing. And Belman still working like a fiend on the Keystone . . . . Even he must have known the Moon Witch wasn't dead, or he wouldn't have kept on with the Keystone, or hurried to get it done before the moon came out again. So Awen-Un really had been the Master Circle after all. And Thorny had saved it. She had moved the forces, she had done the whole thing while he was coming after her, trying to hurt her . . . . His stomach churned. What a fool he had been!

"I didn't know," he said wretchedly. "All those awful things I said—" He turned away. "I called her a . . . and I thought—"

"I know what you thought," Alec said calmly. "Perhaps I ought to have told you the truth earlier. But you're not very good at pretending, Patrick. You have a face that goes right to your soul. I thought if you kept on believing Thorny was a traitor, your behaviour to her would make Belman even more sure that she was someone he could safely disregard. I couldn't afford, at that late date, to let him begin to wonder if the earth-forces might have been moved. That was why I played unconscious, so that at the vital moment he would know that it couldn't have been me. The only person who might have done it was Thorny, but you gave her a good excuse to leave the Circle, and he was so sure of her anyway, it never occurred to him."

A good excuse to leave . . . . In the warm, gentle dark Patrick struggled with anger, with tears of shame. After a moment Alec's hand closed comfortingly on his shoulder. "You made a mistake," he said. "You're human. Don't mind it too much. I think you'll find Thorny has been through enough tonight herself to understand."

"An' it was my 'Arry found 'im there, flatter'n a griddle an' twice as dead, an' tons of rock on 'im. Give me such a turn, 'e did, comin' inter the 'ouse all covered in blood. Wot's that? 'Oo's blood? Why, that man Red's, acourse. 'Arry was drenched in it!"

Aggie Millson settled herself more firmly into her earphones. Same old stuff, only getting bigger and bloodier with each call Millie Hill made. The switchboard was lit up like a Christmas tree. She switched to another call.

"—the moral fibre of this nation." Amelia Green, that was, talking to the police. "When a common thief is found sprawled in a drunken stupor inside what used to be the best house in the parish—"

"We have arrested Alf Sanders ma'am. He's wanted by the police for a number of crimes, but went out of circulation several months ago. Mr. Belman had no idea . . . "

"Mr. Belman didn't know one of his servants was a criminal? Come, come, my man. I should be very surprised if it wasn't for that very reason that he hired this Sanders man in the first place. A man does not surround himself with murderers for nothing."

Aggie nodded to herself. Amelia Green was right. No smoke without fire, *she* always said.

Sergeant Quigley was beginning to sound harassed. "There now, there's no talk of murder, not to my knowledge. The man Red died in a freak accident—"

"And what about Mr. Kingsley? His shooting was a freak accident, too, I suppose? I should hate to attempt to teach you your business, Sergeant, but I do hope you have considered the possibility that this man Sanders did it."

"Naturally we have considered the possibility. Now if you'll excuse me, Miss . . . "

"Oh, and Sergeant."

"Yes?"

"Have you arrested Mr. Belman yet?"

"Certainly not. He has done nothing illegal. In fact, it was he who reported the man Sanders to us—"

164

"A falling out of thieves," Miss Green murmured. "So you let him go?"

Quigley cleared his throat. "Mr. Belman . . . er, must have misunderstood our instructions. Apparently he has decided to . . . er, leave Wychwood Mount. Mannings Estate Agency has been told to put the Hall up for sale. But I'm sure he'll be back for the inquest."

When pigs flew, he would, Aggie thought. Well, nobody in the village would be sorry to see the back end of him and his cement factory. Wychwood Mount had given him more than he'd bargained for, at least. Sent him off, it had, no satisfaction given, and the first earthquake in living memory and the hottest day ever recorded in England to remember it by. She nodded, making herself more comfortable. She could actually feel a breeze. That heat wave had broken at last.

In the garden of the Newports' cottage Alec and Patrick were waiting for Thorny. Patrick felt as if he had been waiting forever. She hadn't yet come home when he and Alec had tiptoed into the house sometime after midnight. Patrick had propped himself against the wall by her door, determined to see her as soon as she got back. But somehow exhaustion had caught up with him, and he'd fallen asleep. He'd wakened when the moon was setting, but her door was shut and locked. Who could blame her? he thought bitterly. He stumbled to his own bed, but the rest of the night could only lie awake and think.

Breakfast had been a silent meal, just him and Alec, with Jenny sleeping peacefully in the blessedly cool morning, and no sign of Thorny. Patrick wanted to knock her door down, but he wrote her a note instead, slipping it under her door with an apologetic tap. "Alec's leaving," the note said. "He wants to say goodbye." And, struggling, he'd added, "I was such an idiot! I wouldn't blame you if you never spoke to me again." And now they were waiting—Alec calmly, Patrick like a cat on hot bricks.

"She's not going to come," he was saying for about the tenth time, when the back door opened and out she came.

23

The Two Whales

Thorny knew what he was feeling; with Patrick you always knew. Hang-dog, he approached, expecting her to be angry, expecting her to hate him. She didn't. She had hated the Moon Witch, a powerful, all-consuming hatred that had left her a murderer in conscience, if not in reality. What other hatred could compare to that?

"Thorny," Patrick said. "Thorny, I'm sorry. I was so stupid, so bloody, bloody stupid!"

"It's okay," Thorny said. "I know. It's over." Over. The peace of it descended like a blessing.

"Don't look like that," Patrick said miserably.

"Like what?"

"Like . . . oh, I don't know, all crumpled or something. A wet tissue, sort of." He stopped, cringing.

"I was actually just feeling relieved," she said, lifting her chin at him. "Not all of my feelings are because of you, you know." Or because of anybody, she thought. And she smiled, the freedom of it lifting her like wings.

"Alec's waiting," Patrick said a bit awkwardly. He felt shy of her, as if she were someone he had to get to know all over again.

And they went together to the old willow where Alec was sitting, peacefully smoking. "What did I tell you?" he said to Patrick, jerking his head at Thorny, who was still faintly smiling. "She knows what it's like to lose control, you see. We all do."

"You, too?"

"Oh, yes. It comes from our dark side. We all have one. But there's no point in giving in to it, not with *them*." Neither Thorny nor Patrick had to ask whom he meant. "The thing is, we can't judge them by human standards. To them we're no more than pawns in their own private little game of chess."

"That's what really got me," Thorny said, her voice low. "Her using me like that. Her having planned everything right from the start. And all that about my father . . . You know, I never saw how much he was like Belman, not until—" She broke off. "Did she actually make Dad the way he is, or did she just choose him?"

"She used him," Alec said. "She can always find uses for people who want to be in control of their world—and for people who refuse to be." He sent her a piercing look, not unkindly. She reddened, looking away. "It's balance that defeats her," he said then. "The courage to make one's own choices without sacrificing the choices of others. But you have learned that lesson." He smiled. "Because you found your own strengths, the Moon Witch couldn't use you at all."

"And I'll bet she's hopping mad about that," Patrick said smugly.

Alec nodded. "She is probably even angrier with Thorny than Belman is with you, and that's saying a lot." Patrick shifted uncomfortably.

"What will they . . . do to us?" Thorny asked.

"As far as what they *can* do, well, in human form, a good deal, I'm afraid. But when they're in human form they *are* human, or mostly so, and you can use their human weaknesses against them. It's in their natural form that they are the most dangerous, even though they cannot actually harm you physically. You see, then they have the power to know you too well, to find your innermost fears and weaknesses and exploit them, to draw you into situations where you can harm yourselves." He nodded at their grave faces. "Yes, they are very much to be feared. But I'm not as afraid for

167

you as I seem. Experience is a hard teacher, but a good one, and a lesson painfully learned is not easily forgotten.''

"*I* won't forget," Patrick said.

"I'm not so sure," Alec said. "You barge into things without thinking, Patrick. It's in your nature. Fortunately you have Thorny, and she has you. It's all very well to be independent—" and he looked directly at Thorny "—but no one is alone in this world, not when one's actions can affect so many others. Respect is the key: for oneself, for each other. Balance, always balance. Remember that, and you will be safe.''

Patrick stretched a little, the sun warm on his face, the moss like a cool green sponge beneath him. Last night with all its dangers seemed a hundred years away. "You don't really think they're going to try to get revenge on us, do you?" he asked.

Alec shrugged. "Who knows? But you must remain constantly on your guard. It might be years before they take action against you. It might even be never. Time means nothing to them, you see. So don't ever forget them. Sun God, Moon Witch—either is a foe dangerous enough for anyone.''

Sun God. Patrick's jaw dropped. "Belman?" he exclaimed. "You don't mean to say Belman is—?"

"Of course. Are you really so surprised? You accepted it easily enough that the lady was Goddess of the Moon."

"That's different. She's . . . well, she's magical. I know Belman wasn't normal, but—" He shivered suddenly, remembering his last moments with Belman in the Circle, those moments when Belman had been anything but normal. More than ever he wished he hadn't been so foolhardy.

"Bel," Alec murmured, "Baal, Beli, Belinus. They are all his names. Ancient God of the Sun. The Moon Witch's son.''

"She was his mother?" Patrick burst out, shocked. "But how could she be? He hates her!"

168

"A parent in charge," Alec shrugged. "A child trying to escape. It happens all the time. But there are escapes and escapes. Sometimes the child becomes what he fights, and then it is no escape at all."

Belman and the Moon Witch, Thorny thought, wondering and sad. Did he love her still, even as he strove to be free of her? As if in a dream she heard again that pain-filled voice of his: *In the end she abandons us all.* For a moment Thorny knew him, for a moment she almost was him. That was the thing, she realized suddenly, that had made her vulnerable to him all this time. It was not that he resembled her father, though he did, in those high cheekbones, in those sure eyes, in the way he made you want to please him. Those were his strengths, those were the qualities the Moon Witch had counted on Thorny rebelling against. But what she hadn't counted on was that Belman had known from his own experience what it was to strive for independence, and what it was to be abandoned. Understanding had given him a stronger grip on Thorny than all the Moon Witch's threats, than all her empty promises of love. Yet even having gone through it all himself, still he had used that understanding of his as a weapon against Thorny, trying to make her worship only him. Belman, her father, the Moon Witch . . . *All is the same, all comes to me in the end.*

But not me, Thorny vowed, never me, never again.

She looked at the Hall, lifeless in the gentle morning. Belman gone, her father gone, her mother a distant stranger. She was alone. The price of independence . . . . And then she saw Alec's eyes on her, warm with understanding, and Patrick running his hands over the moss beneath the tree, and smelled Aunt Jenny's breakfast cooking in the old-fashioned kitchen. Independence didn't mean having to be alone. It only meant having the right to choose.

"Belman is gone, isn't he?" Patrick asked, catching Thorny's look at the Hall.

"Oh, yes, Wychwood Mount has seen the last of him. That trick of Thorny's fooled him completely. It was a brilliant idea to move the earth-powers to the zodiac. It was so obvious, right under his nose, that he never saw it for what it was—a circle with twelve stones: the only possible place anyone might have moved the earth-powers to at such short notice.''

He tapped his pipe out on the ground. "Not that he ever really thought anyone might have moved the powers from Awen-Un. There were clearly earth-forces there, but Belman has been destroying circle after circle for centuries, and all of them have contained some power. He hoped this one would be the Master Circle, but he wasn't sure. When I lay unconscious at his feet, and Thorny was the only one to leave, and she had already proved herself loyal, and as far as he knew couldn't even dowse, *and* had been given a good reason to run away anyway—" Patrick squirmed embarrassedly "—well, in the end, he just had to accept that those few bits of power that had revealed themselves were all there were. Which meant that he had been wrong once again in his quest for the Master Circle." He raised his brows wryly. "Except that this time, he wasn't.''

"Has Belman been the one who's wrecked all the other stone circles?" Thorny asked.

"He's done a lot of it. He hates the circles, because they reduce his power, at the same time as they concentrate the lady's. She, of course, likes the circles for exactly the same reason.''

"Then she doesn't . . . mind . . . that I did save her Master Circle?" Thorny whispered.

"Certainly not. It was your method that she objects to. She wanted you to do it by killing Belman.''

Patrick was frowning. "How do the circles reduce Belman's powers?''

Alec looked at his watch. "A quick explanation will have to do," he said. "The circles were originally a human invention. The people who set them up did it to get help from their goddess the moon to bring the earth-forces under control. They thought, by lining up pairs of stones with the place

170

on the horizon where the moon would rise at special times, a flow of energy would come directly from the moon to the stones. This energy, added to the electromagnetic properties of the stones themselves, would bring the earth-forces under control, do you see?"

Patrick wasn't sure he did, but he didn't want to stop Alec, either. "As far as humans were concerned," Alec went on, "there was no question that the earth-forces had to be controlled. You saw what it was like last night. Multiply it by a million, and you can guess what life was like before the earth-forces were pinned to their network."

He paused. Patrick took a chance. "You still haven't explained why the circles reduced Belman's powers."

"Bel is a sun god. And as you know, a great many of the circles have solar alignments. It occurred by accident at first, a pair of stones in one particular circle just happening to line up with the sunrise at midsummer, when the sun's power was greatest. Then in addition to the Moon Witch's power pouring into her own stones, Bel's sun-power did as well. The power he lost to the circles became the Moon Witch's, because the circles were her domain. And it got worse and worse for Belman, because those circles which had both sun and moon alignments controlled the earth-forces better than the others, and so in the end the ancients built only the dual-purpose kind, and he kept losing more and more of his power to her."

"And so Belman began destroying all the circles," Thorny nodded.

"It was a difficult undertaking," Alec said. "He had to take human form to do it, because the Moon Witch couldn't destroy him that way. But as a human he had to work very slowly at destroying the circles. What with one thing and another, like the kind of protests that happened here when his plans to destroy Awen-Un were revealed, he had been at it for a very long time. Then somehow he learned that there was a Master Circle, the centre of the whole network that

171

controlled the earth-forces. He's been looking for it ever since."

Thorny was regarding Alec thoughtfully. "Alec," she said slowly, "how come you know so much? Where exactly do you fit in?"

Alec looked again at his watch. "I do have to go."

"You can't," Patrick protested. "We'll never know if you don't tell us. How *do* you know so much about the circles and Belman and the Moon Witch and everything? Were you there right from the start?"

The question seemed to hang on the air, taking on a reality Patrick's half-joking voice had never believed possible. He stared at Alec. "Is that why Belman called you the Old One?" he asked slowly.

Alec sighed, putting his pipe away into his pocket. "In the beginning," he said, "there was only heat, flood, earthquake, volcano, fire and misery. Sun God, Moon Witch— what did it matter to humans? Everything was deadly, everything the enemy of life. If human-kind was to have even the slightest chance of surviving, *someone* had to show them what to do."

"Then are you . . . a god, too?" Patrick demanded, half-shy, half-embarrassed.

Alec laughed. "Me? Certainly not. I'm just a poor petty little human like you and Thorny and everybody else. And thank goodness for that!"

"But then?"

"You might say someone like me was there, if you really must know, Patrick. There might even be a fair number of us, one way or another."

"All of you working against Belman?"

Alec shook his head. "It's not what we're against that's important, Patrick. It's what we're for."

"And what are you for?"

"I've told you. People. Life. Balance. No, no more questions, please. My time is almost up. Thorny? My loan to you?"

172

She knew what he meant: the medallion she had been so reluctant to take, the medallion she now would have given anything to have kept. Slowly she lifted it over her head and handed it to him. "Will you be using it again?" she asked.

"Perhaps. You know only one of its uses." His hand closed around it. Patrick leaned forward, staring at the medallion. To him it still looked like an ordinary compass. "I still don't see that symbol," he said sadly.

Alec gave him a look. Then he nodded. "This?" he asked, scratching it on the ground with a twig. "It's the oldest symbol in the world. Perhaps its most common name now is the Two Whales."

"I see them," Thorny said. "One black whale upside-down, one white one rightside-up beside it."

"Yin and yang," Alec nodded, "light and dark, male and female, fire and water. Yes, even the sun and the moon. Each is worth nothing without the other, yet together they are everything. Let the halves struggle how they will, it is the union that triumphs." He got to his feet. "Goodbye, you two," he said. "Keep a watch out for each other."

Patrick cleared his throat. "Will we ever see you again, Alec?"

"Perhaps. Chance is a strange thing."

"When?"

"Not before we need to, at least. Now I really must go." He smiled very gently. "Remember the Two Whales!"

And then he turned and walked away, a tough, white-haired, hawk-nosed man with a job to do.

TO THE READER

There are hundreds of stone circles in England and Scotland, and many more hundreds of isolated standing stones. Many people have tried to explain why these huge standing stones were erected, but no single explanation is universally accepted. To some scientists, like Professors Alexander Thom and Fred Hoyle, the circles were gigantic calendars, designed to mark the passage of the solar year and the much more complex 18.6 year lunar cycle, and even to predict eclipses. A great many stone circles do have pairs of stones that line up with special sunrises or moonrises. It seems most unlikely that this was an accident. Perhaps the people who made these alignments were Stone Age scientists, interested in astronomy for its own sake. It seems more likely, however, that their interest in the positions of the sun and the moon was due to the fact that they did worship them as gods.

Archaeologists tell us that a sun god named Bel (Baal, etc.) was almost universally worshipped, and before him, a goddess who controlled fertility, the moon and death. She had many names according to Robert Graves in his outstanding book *The White Goddess* (Faber and Faber, 1948). I have called her the Moon Witch in this book. Hawthorn was indeed one tree very sacred to this goddess. Also associated with her were stone circles (especially those with twelve stones), owls, mares, cows and sows, the spiral figure, and the numbers three and nine.

The legends mentioned in this book about stones that move by themselves do indeed exist, and there are many more than

174

those stated here. Dowsers do claim that there are earth-currents under most standing stones, and that touching the stones at certain phases of the moon can produce a large electrical shock. Such dowsers, and others, have suggested that the stone circles might have been power generators (used to make life easier in the "golden age" of prehistoric man) or power controllers (as in the lightning rod analogy mentioned in this book). Most scientists do not believe these theories.

Dowsing is an ancient folk-art that has been used through the ages to find underground water, buried treasure and many other things (not all underground). In many cases it appears to work at least as well as modern engineering techniques, though scientists do not understand why, and are generally sceptical of it. Dowsers are sure it works, however. Some say they can even use it to move tiny streams of water together underground, in order to make one really good gusher for a well. An ability to move the earth-forces thus doesn't seem entirely impossible.

Awen-Un doesn't really exist, but many stone circles like it do, and many more have been destroyed through the ages. The greatest of them all, Avebury, was devastated by the fire and water method Belman used on the Keystone in this book. The Ancient Monuments Protection Act exists in Britain to protect stone circles and other old structures nowadays, but it is unfortunately true that on private land ancient monuments which have not been "listed" with the correct governmental department can be (and are being) torn down by their "owners." I am extremely grateful to my father, Robert Wilton, and to Peg Wilton, for researching this situation for me, and for providing many such examples.

I also want to thank the Explorations Program of the Canada Council, whose financial assistance and encouragement helped make this book possible. In addition, I am much indebted to Dr. Don McKay of the Department of English, University of Western Ontario, who read and made helpful comments on the book in its early stages; to Lori Lefebvre,

175

who typed it; to Dr. John Landstreet of the Department of Astronomy, University of Western Ontario, who advised me about eclipses; to my friends Joan Finegan and Kinny Kreiswirth, for their practical help and advice; to my editor, Shelley Tanaka, who kept this book alive when I had almost given up on it; and most of all to my husband, Albert Katz, for his many helpful suggestions, for the hours and hours he gave up so that I could write, for the constancy of his encouragement, and for believing in me. This book is dedicated to him.